THE
WORLD'S
BEST
KARLSON

Also by Astrid Lindgren
Pippi Longstocking
Pippi Goes Aboard
Pippi in the South Seas

Emil's Clever Pig
Emil and the Great Escape
Emil and the Sneaky Rat

Lotta Says, 'No!'
Lotta Makes a Mess

Karlson on the Roof
Karlson Flies Again

ASTRID LINDGREN

THE
WORLD'S
BEST
KARLSON

Translated by Sarah Death • Illustrated by Tony Ross

OXFORD
UNIVERSITY PRESS

OXFORD
UNIVERSITY PRESS

Great Clarendon Street, Oxford OX2 6DP
Oxford University Press is a department of the University of Oxford.
It furthers the University's objective of excellence in research, scholarship,
and education by publishing worldwide in
Oxford   New York
Auckland   Cape Town   Dar es Salaam   Hong Kong   Karachi
Kuala Lumpur   Madrid   Melbourne   Mexico City   Nairobi
New Delhi   Shanghai   Taipei   Toronto
With offices in
Argentina   Austria   Brazil   Chile   Czech Republic   France   Greece
Guatemala   Hungary   Italy   Japan   Poland   Portugal   Singapore
South Korea   Switzerland   Thailand   Turkey   Ukraine   Vietnam
Oxford is a registered trade mark of Oxford University Press
in the UK and in certain other countries

This translation of *The World's Best Karlson* originally published in Swedish
published by arrangement with Saltkråkan Förvaltning AB

The moral rights of the author, illustrator, and translator have been asserted

First published as *Karlsson På Taket Smyger Igen* by Rabén & Sjögren, Sweden 1968
First published in Great Britain by Methuen Children's Books Ltd 1980
First published in this edition 2009 by Oxford University Press

Database right Oxford University Press (maker)

Data available
ISBN: 978-0-19-272773-2

3 5 7 9 10 8 6 4 2

Printed in Great Britain by CPI Cox and Wyman, Reading, Berkshire

Paper used in the production of this book is a natural,
recyclable product made from wood grown in sustainable forests.
The manufacturing process conforms to the environmental
regulations of the country of origin.

CONTENTS

Anybody has the Right to be Karlson   *1*

Karlson Remembers it's his Birthday   *29*

Karlson is the Best in the Class   *59*

Karlson Stays the Night   *77*

Karlson does some Tasty Tirritation   *95*

Karlson is the World's Best Snore Expert   *123*

Karlson Jiggery-pokes Best in the Dark   *145*

Karlson Reveals Fairyland to Uncle Julius   *173*

Karlson is the World's Richest Man   *199*

Anybody has the Right to
be Karlson

One morning Smidge—the youngest and smallest member of the Stevenson family—woke up to the sound of Mum and Dad talking to each other in the kitchen. It sounded almost as if they were cross or upset about something.

'That's torn it,' said Dad. 'Look what it says here in the paper. Here, read this!'

'Oh no, that's terrible,' said Mum, 'Absolutely terrible!'

Smidge leapt straight out of bed. He wanted to know what was so terrible.

Well, he soon found out. On the front page of the paper was the huge headline:

SPYPLANE OR UFO?

And underneath it said:

What is the unidentified flying object seen in the skies over Stockholm? Sightings are reported of a very small, barrel-shaped plane or something of the kind, with a loud, droning motor, flying over the rooftops of the Vasa district. The Board of Civil Aviation denies all knowledge of it and suspects some stealthy little spy is at work, flying around to scout for information. This must be investigated, and the airborne intruder must be captured. If it is a stealthy little spy, he must be handed over to the police without delay.

Who will solve the Stockholm UFO mystery? A reward of ten thousand kronor is on offer for the capture of the droning object, whatever it turns out to be. Anyone turning the thing in to the offices of this newspaper will be able to claim their reward on the spot.

'Poor Karlson on the Roof,' said Mum. 'They'll

give him no peace until they've hunted him down.'

Smidge felt scared and angry and upset, all at the same time.

'Why can't they leave Karlson alone?' he cried. 'He hasn't done any harm. He just lives in his house on the roof and flies around a bit. There's nothing wrong with that, is there?'

'No,' said Dad. 'There's nothing wrong with Karlson. It's just that he's a bit . . . er . . . unusual.'

And there certainly was something unusual about Karlson, even Smidge had to admit that. It *is* unusual to have little, motorized men with folding propellers, and starter buttons on their tummies, living up on the roof in special little houses. Karlson was one of those little men. And Karlson was Smidge's best friend. He was more of a best friend even than Kris and Jemima, who Smidge liked a lot and played with whenever Karlson had gone off somewhere or hadn't got time for him.

Karlson thought Kris and Jemima were a waste of space. Whenever Smidge mentioned their names, he just snorted.

'Don't see how you can talk about those puny shrimps and me in the same breath,' he would say. 'A handsome, thoroughly clever, perfectly plump man in his prime: how many silly little boys have got a best friend like that, eh?'

'Only me,' Smidge would answer, and every time he felt a heart-warming glow of happiness. How lucky he was that Karlson had decided to settle down on *his* roof! The whole Vasa district was full of those unsightly old four-storey blocks of flats like the one the Stevensons lived in, so what luck that Karlson had ended up on their roof and not anybody else's.

Mum and Dad, though, had not been particularly happy about Karlson to start with, and Smidge's brother Seb and sister Sally hadn't liked him at first, either. The whole family—apart from Smidge, of course—thought Karlson was the most dreadful, cheeky, spoilt, meddlesome mischief-maker you could ever imagine. But more recently they had started getting used to him. They almost liked Karlson now, and above all they had realized that Smidge needed him. After all, Seb and Sally were so much older than Smidge, and having no brothers or sisters of about his own age meant he needed a best friend. Admittedly he had his very own dog now, a wonderful little puppy called Bumble, but even that wasn't enough—Smidge needed Karlson.

'And I think Karlson needs Smidge, too,' said Mum.

But right from the start, Mum and Dad had wanted to keep Karlson as secret as possible. They knew what a fuss there would be if the television people, for example, found out about him, or if the weekly magazines sent reporters round to write 'At Home with Karlson' articles.

'Ha ha, it would be hilarious,' Seb said once, 'if they put a photo on the cover of their magazine showing Karlson smelling a bunch of pink roses in his lounge.'

'Don't be stupid,' Smidge had said. 'Karlson hasn't got a lounge, only one crammed-full little room, and no roses either.'

Well, of course, Seb knew that. Once—but only once—he and Sally and Mum and Dad had been up onto the roof to see Karlson's house. They had climbed up through the trapdoor in the attic, the one the chimney sweep used, and Smidge had shown them how cleverly Karlson's house was hidden away behind the chimney stack, tucked up against the wall of the house next door.

Mum had been terrified when she got up onto the roof and saw the street far below. She almost fainted and had to grab hold of the chimney.

'Smidge, promise me never to climb up here on your own,' she said.

Smidge considered this for a while before promising.

'All right,' he said in the end, 'I shan't ever climb up here on my own . . . but I might fly up with Karlson sometimes,' he added in a much quieter voice. If Mum didn't hear that bit, she only had herself to blame. And anyway, how could she ask Smidge never to visit Karlson? She obviously had no idea how much fun you could have in Karlson's crammed-full little room, where there was so much stuff.

But now it would all have to stop, thought

Smidge bitterly, just because of that stupid newspaper article.

'You'd better tell Karlson to watch out,' said Dad. 'He'd better not go flying around quite so openly for a while. You can play with him in your room, where no one will see him.'

'But I shall kick him out if he gets up to too much mischief,' said Mum.

She brought Smidge's porridge over to him at the kitchen table, and gave Bumble a little helping in his dog bowl. Dad said goodbye and went off to the office. And it turned out Mum had to go out for a while, too.

'I'm just popping down to the travel agent's to see if there are any nice holidays on offer, since Dad's got some time off coming up,' she said, and gave Smidge a kiss. 'I'll be back soon.'

So Smidge was left alone. Alone with Bumble and his porridge and his thoughts. And the newspaper. It was lying beside him and he glanced over at it from time to time. Under the story about Karlson there was a lovely picture of a big, white steamer that had put into Stockholm and dropped anchor at one of the quaysides. Smidge looked at it. Oh, he did think it looked nice, and he wished very much that he could see a boat like that in real life, and sail off across the sea in it!

He tried not to see anything but the boat. But his eyes kept straying to that horrible headline:

SPYPLANE OR UFO?

Smidge was seriously worried. He would have to speak to Karlson as soon as possible. But he mustn't alarm him too much, because what if Karlson was so scared that he flew away and never came back?

Smidge sighed. Then he reluctantly put a spoonful of porridge into his mouth. He didn't swallow the porridge, but held it experimentally on his tongue. Smidge was one of those scrawny little boys with poor appetites that there are so many of. He always sat picking at his food, so it took him forever to finish.

No, he really didn't like porridge very much, Smidge decided. Maybe it would taste better with more sugar on it. He was just picking up the

sugar basin when he heard the buzz of a motor outside the kitchen window, and hey presto, in flew
Karlson.

'Heysan hopsan, Smidge,' he cried, 'guess who's the
world's bestest best friend, and guess why he's here.'

Smidge quickly swallowed what he had in his
mouth.

'The world's bestest best friend is you, Karlson!
But why are you here?'

'Three guesses,' said Karlson. 'Because I was missing you, you silly little boy, or because I took a

wrong turning when I really meant to go for a fly round the city park, or because I could smell porridge? Start guessing!'

Smidge cheered up and his face brightened.

'Because you were missing me,' he suggested shyly.

'Wrong,' said Karlson. 'And I wasn't heading for the city park either, so don't bother guessing that.'

The city park, thought Smidge, oh no! Karlson simply mustn't go flying there, or anywhere else where there were loads of people to see him. Smidge would have to explain.

'Listen, Karlson,' he began, but then he stopped, because he suddenly noticed Karlson was looking very grumpy. He was pouting and giving Smidge a sullen stare.

'A person turns up starving hungry,' he said, 'but does anyone pull up a chair for them and fetch a bowl for them and tie a napkin under their chin and give them a big helping of porridge and tell them they've got to have a spoonful for Mummy and a spoonful for Daddy and a spoonful for Aunt Augusta . . . ?'

'Who's Aunt Augusta?' asked Smidge curiously.

'No idea,' said Karlson.

'Well, you don't need to have a spoonful for her then, do you!' laughed Smidge.

But Karlson wasn't laughing.

'Is that right? So a person's meant to starve to death, are they, just because they don't happen to know all the aunts in the world who might be sitting twiddling their thumbs in Tumbarumba or Timbuktu, or wherever they are?'

Smidge quickly got out another bowl and invited Karlson to help himself from the porridge saucepan. Still rather grumpy, Karlson poured some into his bowl. He poured and poured, and finished by running his finger round the pan to scrape it clean.

'Your mum's very nice,' said Karlson, 'but it's a shame she's so terribly stingy. I've seen a lot of porridge in my time, but never as little as this.'

He emptied the entire contents of the sugar basin over his porridge and tucked in. For several minutes the only sound in the kitchen was the sort of slurping you get when someone is eating porridge at high speed.

'I'm afraid there wasn't enough for a spoonful for Aunt Augusta,' said Karlson, wiping his mouth. 'But I see there are some buns! Easy now, take it easy, little Aunt Augusta, just you relax down there in Tumbarumba. I can always force down a couple of buns for you instead. Or even three . . . or four . . . or five!'

While Karlson wolfed down buns, Smidge sat brooding about how to warn him. Perhaps the best thing would be to let him read it for himself, thought Smidge, and timidly pushed the newspaper across to Karlson.

'Look at the front page,' he said grimly, and Karlson did. He looked at it with great interest, and then stabbed at the picture of the white steamer with a pudgy little finger.

'Dear dear, another boat's capsized,' he said. 'It's just one disaster after another!'

'No, you're just holding the paper upside down,' Smidge pointed out.

Smidge had suspected for some time that Karlson wasn't much good at reading. But he was a kindly little soul who didn't want to upset anybody, least of all Karlson, so he didn't say: 'Ha ha, you can't read, can you?' but just turned the paper and the boat picture the right way up, so Karlson could see there hadn't been a disaster at sea.

'But there's plenty here about other disasters,' said Smidge. 'Listen to this!'

Then he read out the piece about the barrel-shaped spyplane and the stealthy little spy who had got to be captured and the reward and everything.

'All people have to do is turn the thing in to the offices of this newspaper, and they can claim their reward money on the spot,' he ended with a sigh.

But Karlson wasn't sighing, he was cheering.

'Whoop, whoop!' he shouted, with a couple of eager, joyous little jumps into the air. 'Whoop, whoop, the stealthy little spy is as good as caught. Ring the offices of this newspaper and tell them I'll be turning the thing in this very afternoon!'

'What do you mean?' asked Smidge in horror.

'The world's best spy catcher, guess who that is?' said Karlson, pointing proudly to himself.

'Yours truly, when I come dashing with my big butterfly net. If that stealthy little spy is flying around in this neighbourhood, I shall have him in my net before the day's out, you can be sure of that . . . by the way, have you got a rucksack or something, that I can fit ten thousand kronor in?'

Smidge sighed again. This was going to be even more difficult than he had thought. Karlson hadn't grasped the problem at all.

'Oh, Karlson, you must realize it's you who's the barrel-shaped spyplane; it's you they want to catch, don't you see?'

Karlson suddenly lost his bounce. He made a gurgling sound as if there was something caught in his throat, and glared at Smidge in fury.

'Barrel-shaped!' he shrieked. 'Are you calling me barrel-shaped? And we're supposed to be best friends. Huh, thank you *very* much!'

He stood up as straight as he could, to make himself taller, and pulled in his tummy as far as it would go.

'Perhaps you haven't noticed,' he said loftily,

'that I am a handsome and thoroughly clever and perfectly plump man in my prime. Perhaps you haven't noticed that, eh?'

'Of course I have, Karlson, of course I have,' stuttered Smidge. 'But I can't help what they write in the papers, can I? It's you they mean, I'm absolutely sure of it.'

Karlson was getting more and more worked up.

'All people have to do is turn the thing in to the offices of this newspaper,' he yelled bitterly. 'The thing,' he yelled. 'Anyone who calls me "the thing" will get a big enough biff between the eyes to send his nose flying.'

He made a couple of threatening little lunges at Smidge, but he shouldn't have done that, because it made Bumble leap up. Bumble had no intention of letting anyone come and shout at his master.

'Down, Bumble, leave Karlson alone,' said Smidge, and Bumble did as he was told. He just growled a bit to make sure Karlson understood he meant business.

Karlson flopped glumly down onto a stool in a bad fit of the sulks.

'You can count me out,' he said. 'You can count me out, if you're just going to be horrid all the time and call me "the thing" and set your bloodhounds on me.'

Smidge was quite shaken. He didn't know what to say or do.

'I honestly can't help what's in the paper, you know,' he mumbled. Then he stopped. Karlson wasn't saying anything either. He sat on his stool, sulking, and there was a depressing silence in the kitchen.

Then Karlson gave a sudden roar of laughter. He

leapt up from the stool and gave Smidge a playful little punch in the stomach.

'But if I'm a thing,' he said, 'at least I'm the world's best thing, worth ten thousand kronor, had you thought of that?'

Smidge started laughing, too, because it was great to see Karlson in a good mood again.

'Yes, so you are,' said Smidge happily, 'you're worth ten thousand kronor, and I'm sure not many people are.'

'Nobody in the whole wide world,' declared Karlson. 'A puny little thing like you, say, can't be worth more than a kronor twenty-five at most, I bet you.'

He turned his winder and rose jubilantly into the air, and then flew a lap of honour round the ceiling light, hooting with delight.

'Whoop, whoop,' he went, 'here comes Ten Thousand Kronor Karlson, whoop, whoop!'

Smidge decided not to worry about anything any more. Karlson really wasn't a spy, after all, and the police couldn't arrest him just for being Karlson. He suddenly realized that wasn't what Mum and Dad were afraid of, either. They were only worried that they wouldn't be able to keep Karlson a secret any longer, if he was going to be hunted down with such a hue and cry. But surely nothing really bad could happen to him, Smidge thought.

'You needn't be frightened, Karlson,' he said consolingly. 'They can't do anything to you just for being you.'

'No, absolutely anybody has the right to be Karlson,' Karlson declared. 'Though so far there's only the one first-rate, perfectly plump specimen.'

They were back in Smidge's room by then, and Karlson was looking round hopefully.

'Have you got a steam engine we can explode or something else that goes off with a good bang? It's got to go bang and I've got to have fun, otherwise you can count me out,' he said, but at that moment he caught sight of the paper bag on Smidge's table, and pounced on it like a hawk. Mum had put it there the evening before. There was a lovely big peach inside, and that glossy peach was now in the grip of Karlson's pudgy fingers.

'We can share,' suggested Smidge quickly. He liked peaches too, you see, and he realized he'd need to be quick to get a taste of this one.

'By all means,' said Karlson. 'We'll share: I'll have the peach and you can have the bag. That means you get the best bit, because there's all sorts of fun you can have with a paper bag.'

'Ohnothanks,' gabbled Smidge, 'we'll share the peach, then you're welcome to have the bag.'

Karlson shook his head disapprovingly.

'Never seen such a greedy little boy,' he said. 'All right, whatever you like!'

They needed a knife to cut the peach in half, and Smidge ran off to the kitchen to get one. When he got back, there was no sign of Karlson. But then Smidge discovered him sitting under the table, almost out of sight, and heard an eager slurping, the sort you get when someone is eating a juicy peach at high speed.

'Hey, what are you doing?' asked Smidge anxiously.

'Sharing,' said Karlson. There was one last guzzling noise and then Karlson came crawling out with peach juice running down his chin. He held out a podgy hand to Smidge and passed him a wrinkled brown peach stone.

'I always want you to have the best bit,' he said. 'If you plant this stone, you'll get a whole peach tree stuffed full of peaches. You've got to admit I'm the world's kindest Karlson, not making a fuss even though I only got one miserable little peach!'

Before Smidge could admit anything, Karlson had darted over to the window, where there was a pink geranium in a pot on the sill.

'And being kind like I am, I shall help you plant it as well,' he said.

'Stop!' yelled Smidge. But it was too late. Karlson had already uprooted the geranium from its pot, and before Smidge could stop him, he threw it out of the window.

'You're crazy,' began Smidge, but Karlson wasn't listening.

'A whole big peach tree! Think of that! At your fiftieth birthday party you'll be able to give every single guest a peach for dessert, won't that be nice?'

'Maybe, but it won't be so nice when Mum finds out you've pulled up her geranium,' said Smidge.

'And if it's fallen on the head of some old man down in the street, what do you think he's going to say?'

'Thank you kindly, Karlson, he'll say,' declared Karlson. 'Thank you kindly for pulling up the geranium and not throwing it out pot and all . . . which Smidge's daft mum thinks is a great idea.'

'Oh no she doesn't,' protested Smidge. 'And anyway, what do you mean?'

Karlson pushed the stone into the pot and eagerly heaped soil over it.

'Oh yes she does,' he assured Smidge. 'As long as the geranium's firmly in its pot, she's happy, your mum. She doesn't care that it's deadly dangerous for little old men down in the street. One old man more or less, that's a mere trifle, she says, as long as nobody pulls up my geranium.'

He fixed Smidge with a stare.

'But if I'd thrown out the flowerpot, too, where were you thinking we'd plant the peach stone, eh?'

Smidge hadn't thought anything at all, so he couldn't answer. It was hard making Karlson see sense when Karlson was in this sort of mood. But luckily he was only in this sort of mood once every quarter of an hour or so, and all of a sudden he gave a contented chuckle.

'We've still got the bag,' he said. 'There's all sorts of fun you can have with a paper bag.'

Smidge had never noticed this.

'How?' he asked. 'What can you do with a paper bag?'

Karlson's eyes began to sparkle.

'Make the world's most enormous pop,' he said. 'Whoop, whoop, what a pop! And that's exactly what I'm going to do now!'

He picked up the bag and dashed off with it to the bathroom. Smidge followed him curiously. He very much wanted to know how you make the world's most enormous pop.

Karlson was bending over the bath, filling the bag with water from the tap.

'You're bonkers,' said Smidge. 'Filling a paper bag with water will never work, you must know that.'

'What's this, then?' asked Karlson, holding the

bulging bag under Smidge's nose. He kept it there for a moment to show Smidge that yes, you could fill a paper bag with water, but then he sprinted back to Smidge's room, clutching the bag.

Smidge dashed after him, suspecting the worst. And sure enough . . . Karlson was hanging out of the window, so all you could see was his round backside and his fat little legs.

'Whoop, whoop,' he shouted. 'Mind out below, because here comes the world's most enormous pop!'

'Stop!' yelled Smidge, and quickly leant out of the window himself. 'No, Karlson, no!' he cried anxiously. But it was too late. The bag was already on its way down. Smidge saw it falling like a bomb right at the feet of a poor woman who was on her way to the little shop next door, and she wasn't impressed by the world's most enormous pop, that was very clear.

'She's howling as if it was a flowerpot,' said Karlson. 'And it's only a drop of ordinary water.'

Smidge pulled the window shut sharply. He didn't want Karlson throwing anything else out.

'I don't think you should do things like that,' he said sternly. But that made Karlson roar with laughter. He flew a little circuit of the ceiling light and squinted down at Smidge, sniggering.

'I don't think you should do things like that,' he said, mimicking Smidge. 'How do you think I should do them, then? Fill the bag with rotten eggs, hm? Is that another one of your mum's weird ideas?'

He flew in to land with a thud at Smidge's feet.

'You really are the world's weirdest pair, you and your mum,' he said, and patted Smidge on the cheek. 'But I still like you, oddly enough.'

Smidge went pink with pleasure. After all, it was

wonderful that Karlson liked him, and that he approved of Mum too, although it didn't always sound that way.

'Yes, I'm surprised at myself,' said Karlson. He carried on patting Smidge. He kept at it, gradually patting harder and harder. In the end, Karlson gave Smidge a pat that felt more like a clip round the ear, and announced:

'Ooh, I'm so nice! I'm the world's nicest Karlson. So I think we'll play something really nice now, don't you?'

Smidge agreed, and he immediately started thinking: what nice games were there that you could play with Karlson?

'For example,' said Karlson, 'we could play that your table over there is our raft, for rescuing ourselves when the great flood comes . . . and here it comes now!'

He pointed to a trickle of water coming under the door.

Smidge gasped.

'Didn't you turn off the tap in the bath?' he asked, horrified.

Karlson put his head on one side and looked meekly at Smidge.

'Three guesses if I did or not.'

Smidge opened the door to the hall, and found Karlson was right. The great flood had started. The water covering the hall and bathroom was deep enough to paddle in, if you wanted to.

And Karlson did. He took a delighted jump, feet together, right into the water.

'Whoop, whoop,' he said. 'Some days it's just one lot of fun after another.'

But Smidge, once he had turned off the tap and pulled the plug out of the overflowing bath, sank down on a chair in the hall and looked at the mess in despair.

'Oh dear,' he said, 'whatever will Mum say?'

Karlson stopped jumping, and looked indignantly at Smidge.

'Now wait a minute,' he said, 'how grumpy can she be, your mum? It's only a drop of ordinary water!'

He jumped again, sending water splashing over Smidge.

'Rather nice water, actually,' he said. 'Look, everyone gets a free footbath. Doesn't she like foot-baths, your mum?'

He did another jump, spraying Smidge even more.

'Doesn't she *ever* wash her feet? Does she spend *all* her days chucking flowerpots, one after another?'

Smidge didn't answer. He had other things on his mind. Then he suddenly realized the urgency of the situation: help, they needed to mop up as quickly as possible, before Mum got home.

'Karlson, we'd better hurry . . . ' he said, leaping to his feet. He darted off to the kitchen and was soon back with a couple of floor cloths.

'Karlson, come and help . . . ' he began. There was no Karlson to be found. No Karlson in the bathroom, or the hall, or in Smidge's room either. But Smidge could hear the whirr of a motor outside. He ran to the window just in time to see something the shape of a fat sausage go whizzing past.

'Spyplane or UFO?' muttered Smidge.

Neither! Just Karlson on his way home to his green house on the roof.

But then Karlson caught sight of Smidge. He went into a steep dive and came swooping past the window with the wind whistling about his ears. Smidge waved frantically with the floor cloth and Karlson waved back with his podgy little hand.

'Whoop, whoop,' he yelled. 'Here comes Ten Thousand Kronor Karlson, whoop, whoop!'

And then he was gone. Smidge went back to the hall with a floor cloth in each hand, to start mopping up.

KARLSON REMEMBERS IT'S HIS BIRTHDAY

It was just as well for Karlson that he was gone by the time Mum got back from the travel agent's, because sure enough she was very cross indeed, not only about the geranium but also about the flood, even though Smidge had managed to mop up most of it.

Mum knew straight away who had been causing such havoc, and she told Dad all about it when he came home for dinner.

'I know it's wrong of me,' said Mum, 'because I have more or less started getting used to Karlson, but *sometimes* I feel as though I'd be happy to pay ten thousand kronor myself, just to be rid of him.'

'Oh, Mum, *no!*' said Smidge.

'Well anyway, we won't say any more about it now,' said Mum, 'because mealtimes are supposed to be pleasant.'

That was what Mum always said: 'Mealtimes are supposed to be pleasant.' Smidge agreed with her. And pleasant it certainly was when they sat round the table eating together and talked about all sorts of things. Smidge talked more than he ate, or at least he did whenever it was boiled cod or vegetable soup or herring balls. But today they were having veal chops and strawberries, and that was because the summer holidays had just started and because Seb and Sally were going away, Seb on a sailing course and Sally to a riding centre on a farm. So that meant they had to have a little farewell party, of course. Mum liked arranging little celebration meals for them every now and then.

'But don't be down in the dumps, Smidge,' said Dad. 'We're going away on holiday too, you and Mum and me.'

And then he told them the exciting news. At the travel agent's, Mum had booked tickets for a cruise on a steamer just like the one Smidge had seen in the paper. They would be leaving in a week's time, and then they'd spend two weeks cruising around on the white boat, stopping at all sorts of harbours and towns. Wouldn't that be fun? asked Mum. Asked Dad. Asked Seb and Sally . . . 'Won't that be really good fun, Smidge?'

'Yes,' said Smidge, and thought it might well turn out to be good fun. But he also sensed there was something not so good about it, and he knew at once what it was—Karlson! How could he leave him all alone, just when Karlson needed him? Smidge had had plenty of time to think about it, I can tell you, while he was mopping up the great flood. Even though Karlson wasn't a spy but just plain Karlson, awful things could still happen once people started chasing him and trying to earn ten thousand kronor from him. Who knows what they might do; maybe they'd put Karlson on show in a cage at the zoo at Skansen or dream up some other terrible fate for him. In any case, they wouldn't just let him stay in his little house on the roof, that was for sure.

Smidge decided he'd have to stay at home and keep an eye on Karlson. And he explained it all in detail as he sat there at the dinner table, gnawing the meat off his chop bone.

Seb started to laugh.

'Karlson in a cage at Skansen zoo . . . wow! Just imagine, Smidge, when you and your class are there on a school trip, and you're wandering round looking at the animals and reading the signs. Polar bear, you'll read, and elk and wolf and beaver and Karlson.'

'Shut up,' said Smidge.

Seb sniggered.

'Please do not feed the Karlson—think how cross Karlson would be if it said that!'

'You're stupid,' said Smidge. 'You really are!'

'But, Smidge,' said Mum, 'if you don't want to come with us, we can't go either, you know that.'

'Of course you can,' said Smidge. 'Karlson and me can do the cooking and cleaning and stuff together.'

'Oh yeah,' said Sally. 'And flood the whole block

of flats, I suppose? And throw all the furniture out of the window?'

'You're stupid,' said Smidge.

This mealtime was having trouble being as pleasant as mealtimes usually were. Although Smidge was such a nice, kindly little boy, he could sometimes be very stubborn. He had made his mind up and wasn't going to listen to anyone trying to persuade him otherwise.

'Come on, mate . . . ' began Dad. He didn't get any further, because there was the sound of something dropping through the letterbox. Sally left the table without even asking; she was expecting letters from various floppy-haired boys. That was why she was in such a tearing hurry to be first out into the hall. And sure enough, there was a letter on the doormat, but it wasn't to Sally from a floppy-haired boy . . . just the opposite. It was to Dad from Uncle Julius, who had no hair at all.

'Mealtimes are supposed to be pleasant,' said Seb. 'That means no letters from Uncle Julius are allowed.'

Uncle Julius was a distant relation of Dad's, and

once a year he would come to Stockholm to see his doctor and visit the Stevensons. Uncle Julius never wanted to stay in a hotel; he thought it was far too expensive. Actually he had loads of money, but he was very careful how he spent it.

Nobody in the Stevenson family was ever very keen on having Uncle Julius to stay. Least of all Dad. But Mum always said:

'You're the only family he's got, after all, and I feel sorry for him. We must be kind to poor Uncle Julius.'

Though by the time Mum had had poor Uncle Julius in the house for a few days, and he had spent the whole time making comments about her children and being fussy about his food and complaining about absolutely everything, Mum would get a frown line in the middle of her forehead and go just as quiet and peculiar as Dad did as soon as Uncle Julius stepped through the front door. And Seb and Sally kept out of the way and were hardly ever at home while Uncle Julius was staying.

'Smidge is the only one who manages to be a bit nice to him,' Mum always said. But even Smidge got tired of it sooner or later, and on Uncle Julius's last visit Smidge had done a picture of him on his drawing pad and written underneath: He's stupid.

Uncle Julius happened to see it, and he said:

'That's not a very good horse!'

No, well, Uncle Julius didn't think *anything* was very good. He most definitely wasn't an easy guest to have about the place, and when he finally packed his bag and headed back home across Sweden to Västergötland, it was as if the whole house blossomed and started singing a happy little tune, Smidge thought. Everyone was giggly and in high spirits, as if something really exciting had happened, when in fact it was only that poor Uncle Julius had gone.

But now he was coming, the letter said, and staying for at least a fortnight, which would be tolerably pleasant, he wrote, and what was more, his doctor had said he needed treatments and massages, because his whole body felt so stiff in the mornings.

'Hah, so much for our cruise,' said Mum. 'Smidge doesn't want to come, and now Uncle Julius will be here!'

But Dad thumped his fist on the table and said he was going on the cruise anyway, and taking Mum with him, even if he had to kidnap her first. Smidge could come with them or stay at home, whichever he liked, take your pick, and Uncle Julius could come and stay in the flat and go to the doctor's as often as he wanted, or stay in Västergötland if he preferred, but as for Dad, he was going on the cruise even if ten Uncle Juliuses turned up, so there!

'Well in that case,' said Mum, 'there's some thinking to be done.'

And when she had finished thinking, she said she would ask that Miss Crawley, who had helped them

when Mum was ill last autumn, if she could come back as home help for a while . . . for two stubborn old bachelors: in other words Smidge and Uncle Julius.

'Plus a certain other stubborn old bachelor by

36

the name of Karlson on the Roof,' said Dad. 'Don't forget Karlson, because he'll be flitting in and out all day long.'

Seb was in such stitches that he almost fell off his chair.

'Creepy Crawley and Uncle Julius and Karlson on the Roof, what a cosy houseful they'll make!'

'And Smidge in the middle of it all, don't forget him,' said Sally.

She took Smidge by the shoulders and looked him straight in the eye.

'Just imagine there being people like my little brother,' she mused. 'He'd rather stay at home with Creepy Crawley and Uncle Julius and Karlson on the Roof than go on a lovely cruise with Mum and Dad.'

Smidge twisted free.

'If you've got a best friend, you jolly well have to look after him,' he said morosely.

Did they think he didn't realize what a bother it was going to be? A huge bother, in fact, what with Karlson flapping round Uncle Julius's and Miss Crawley's ears; oh yes, it was obvious someone had to stay at home and sort out all the trouble.

'And it's got to be me, Bumble, you see,' said Smidge. He was in bed by then, and Bumble was snuffling in his basket alongside.

Smidge stretched down a finger and scratched Bumble under the collar.

'We'd better get some sleep now,' he said, 'so we're ready for all this.'

But then he heard the unexpected buzz of a motor, and in flew Karlson.

'Well, this is a sorry story,' he said. 'I'm supposed to think of everything myself. Nobody helps me remember, oh no!'

Smidge sat up in bed.

'Remember what?'

'That it's my birthday today! It's been my birthday all day long and I didn't remember, because nobody's wished me "Many Happy Returns".'

'But how can it be your birthday on the eighth of June?' asked Smidge. 'I mean, you had your birthday just before Easter, didn't you?'

'Yes, but that was then,' said Karlson. 'And there's simply no need to stick with the same old birthday all the time, when there are so many to choose from. The eighth of June's a good date for a birthday, so do you have to make such a fuss about it?'

Smidge laughed.

'No, it's fine by me for you to have your birthday whenever you like.'

'In that case,' said Karlson, putting his head on one side and giving Smidge an appealing look, 'I'd like my presents now.'

Smidge climbed out of bed, thinking hard. It wasn't easy to come up with a suitable present for Karlson just like that, but he'd try.

'I'll have to have a look in my drawers,' he said.

'You do that,' said Karlson, settling down to wait.

But then he caught sight of the flowerpot where he'd planted the peach stone, and pounced on it. He wiggled his finger down into the soil and prised out the peach stone without further ado.

'I've got to check how much it's grown,' he said. 'Oooh, it's grown a lot, I think.'

Then just as quickly he stuffed the stone back in again, and wiped the soil off his fingers on Smidge's pyjamas.

'You'll have a grand time in ten or twenty years,' he said.

'How do you mean?' asked Smidge.

'You'll be able to take your after-dinner nap in the shade of the peach tree, which is lucky for you, isn't it, because you'll have to chuck out the bed, of course. No room for furniture when you've got peach trees . . . Well, have you found me a present?'

Smidge held out one of his model cars, but Karlson shook his head; the car wouldn't do.

One by one, Smidge tried a jigsaw, a board game,

and a bag of marbles, but Karlson shook his head at them all. Then it dawned on Smidge what Karlson really wanted—his pistol! It was right at the back of the right-hand drawer, in a matchbox. It was the world's smallest toy pistol and the world's best, too. Dad had brought it back for Smidge from one of his trips abroad, and Kris and Jemima had been jealous for days, because nobody had ever seen anything like it before. It looked just like a proper pistol, although it was so tiny, and when you fired it, it went off with a bang just as loud as you get from a proper pistol. It was incredible, Dad said, how loud a bang it could make.

'You'll have to be careful,' he said as he put the little pistol in Smidge's hand. 'You mustn't go around scaring the life out of people with it.'

For various reasons, Smidge hadn't shown Karlson the pistol. He knew it was a bit mean of him, and anyway it hadn't helped, because yesterday Karlson had found it when he was busy rooting around in Smidge's desk drawers.

Karlson had agreed that it was a very fine pistol. Maybe that was why he was having his birthday today, thought Smidge, and with a little sigh he fetched out the matchbox.

'Happy birthday,' he said.

Karlson gave a hoot before rushing up to Smidge and kissing him hard on both cheeks. Then he opened the matchbox and grabbed the pistol with a chortle.

'The world's bestest best friend, that's you, Smidge,' he said, and that made Smidge suddenly feel as happy as a hundred pistols, and he felt with all his heart that he didn't begrudge Karlson this puny little specimen, since Karlson clearly liked it so much.

'You see,' said Karlson, 'I need it, I really do. I need it in the evenings.'

'What for?' asked Smidge uneasily.

'When I'm lying there counting sheep,' said Karlson.

Karlson sometimes used to moan about how badly he slept.

'At nights I sleep like a log,' he would say, 'and in the mornings. But in the afternoons I just lie there tossing and turning, and sometimes I can't get to sleep in the evenings either.'

So Smidge had taught him a useful trick. If you couldn't get to sleep, you could close your eyes and pretend you could see a flock of sheep jumping over a fence. You had to count each sheep just as it jumped, and that made you sleepy, and before you knew it, you had dozed off.

'I couldn't get off to sleep this evening, see,' said Karlson, 'so I lay there counting sheep. But there was one naughty little sheep that wouldn't jump, oh no, it just wouldn't,' said Karlson.

Smidge laughed.

'Why wouldn't it jump?'

'Just to be a pesky nuisance,' said Karlson. 'It stood there by the fence sulking, and simply refused to jump. So then I thought: if I had a bistol, I'd soon teach you how to jump all right. And then I remembered you had a bistol in your desk drawer, Smidge, and then I remembered it was my birthday,' said Karlson, patting the pistol delightedly.

Then Karlson wanted to test his birthday present.

'It's got to go bang and I've got to have fun, otherwise you can count me out.'

But Smidge said no.

'Not on your life! You'll wake the whole house.'

Karlson shrugged.

'Well, that's a mere trifle! They can go back to sleep, can't they? If they haven't got any sheep of their own to count, they can borrow some of mine.'

But Smidge still wouldn't let him fire the pistol, and then Karlson had an idea.

'Let's fly up to my place,' he said. 'I've got to have a birthday party, by the way . . . is there any cake?'

Smidge had to admit there wasn't any cake, and when Karlson grumbled, Smidge told him it was a mere trifle, after all.

'Cake is not a mere trifle,' said Karlson sternly. 'But I suppose we'll have to make do with buns. Go and get as many as you can find.'

So Smidge crept into the kitchen and came back with a passable pile of buns. Mum had given him permission from now on to give Karlson buns whenever the need arose. And the need had certainly arisen now.

On the other hand, Mum had never given him permission to fly up to the roof with Karlson, but Smidge had forgotten that, and he would have been amazed if anyone had reminded him. Smidge was so used to flying with Karlson that he felt calm and safe and didn't even get butterflies in his tummy as he went soaring out of the window with his arms clamped round Karlson and whirred away to Karlson's little house on the roof.

* * *

June evenings in Stockholm are like nothing else in the entire world. Nowhere else does the sky shimmer with such a strange light, nowhere else is the dusk so lovely and magical and blue. And in that blue dusk the city sits on its pale waters as if it has floated up out of some old fairytale and isn't real at all.

Evenings like those are just made for bun feasts on Karlson's porch steps. Smidge generally didn't notice the light in the sky or magical dusks, and as for Karlson, he couldn't have cared less about them. But now, as they sat there enjoying their squash and buns, Smidge at any rate felt that this was an evening not like any other evening. And Karlson felt that Mum's buns were not like any other buns.

Karlson's little house certainly wasn't like any other house in the world either, thought Smidge. There couldn't possibly be such a handy little cottage with such a great location and such a view anywhere else, and there couldn't be such a collection of bits and bobs anywhere else either. Karlson was like a squirrel: he stuffed his nest full. Smidge had no idea where he came by it all, and new things kept appearing. Karlson hung most of them on the wall so he'd be able to find things when he needed them.

'The bits have to go on the left and the bobs on the right,' Karlson had explained to Smidge. In among all his bits and bobs, Karlson also had two nice paintings that Smidge admired. One was of a cockerel and called 'Portrait of a Very Lonely Red Cockerel'; the other was of a fox, and called 'Portrait of my Rabbits'. You couldn't see the rabbits, admittedly, but that was only because they were in the fox, according to Karlson.

'When I get time I'm going to paint one called "Portrait of a Naughty Little Sheep That Refuses to Jump",' declared Karlson, his mouth full of bun.

But Smidge was scarcely listening. The sounds and scents of the summer evening were flowing over him, making him almost giddy. He could smell the scent of the lime trees in flower, all along the street, and hear the tip-tap of heels on the pavement far below, where people were out for a stroll this lovely June evening, and that tip-tapping seemed so summery to Smidge. From the houses all around them came voices; it was such a still evening and every sound could be clearly heard: people talking and singing and quarrelling and shouting and laughing and crying by turns, and having no idea there was a boy sitting up on the roof, listening to it all as if it was some sort of music.

 No, they've no idea that I'm sitting here with Karlson, having a good time and eating buns, thought Smidge with satisfaction.

There was much noisy hooting and bellowing coming from an attic window a bit further along.

'Listen to my thuggy thieves,' said Karlson.

'Your what . . . ? You don't mean Spike and Rollo?' asked Smidge.

'Well, I haven't got any other thuggy thieves, as far as I know.'

Smidge knew Spike and Rollo, too. They were the worst thugs in the neighbourhood and a real pair of thieving magpies. That was why Karlson called them thuggy thieves. One evening last year, they had broken into the Stevensons' flat to burgle it, but Karlson had played ghost and scared them so witless that they probably still hadn't forgotten it. And that time they left without taking anything, not so much as one silver spoon.

But now, when he heard Spike and Rollo letting off steam in their attic, Karlson stood up and brushed off the bun crumbs.

'I think it's a good idea to give them a fright every now and then,' he said. 'Otherwise they only go out grabbing stuff that isn't theirs.'

And he darted off across the rooftops to the attic window. Smidge had never seen anyone with such short legs run so fast. Absolutely anybody would have found it hard to keep up, and Smidge simply wasn't used to running across roofs, but he trotted off after Karlson as quickly as he could.

'Thuggy thieves are real terrors,' said Karlson as he ran. 'If I grab anything, I pay five öre for it straight away, because I'm the world's most honest Karlson. But my five öre coins are nearly all gone now, and I don't know where I'm supposed to grab a new lot from.'

Spike and Rollo had their window open, but the curtains were closed, and from behind them you could hear the pair laughing and bawling their heads off.

'Right, let's see what's so funny,' said Karlson, making a little gap between the curtains to look through. He let Smidge look, too, and they could see Spike and Rollo in their messy room. They were lying on their stomachs on the floor with a newspaper spread out in front of them, and it was something they had read there that was making them so excited.

'Ten thousand. Well, I'll be blowed,' cried Rollo.

'And he's flying round this very neighbourhood.

Well, you could knock me down with a feather,'
cried Spike, positively clucking with laughter.

'Hey, Spike,' said Rollo, 'I know someone who's
planning on earning ten thousand kronor very soon,
ha ha ha!'

'Hey, Rollo,' said Spike, 'I know someone like
that, too, and he's planning on catching a stealthy
little foreign spy, ho ho ho.'

Smidge went pale with fright when he heard
what they were saying, but Karlson sniggered.

'And I know someone who's planning on a bit of
jiggery-pokery right now,' he said, and fired off a
pistol shot. The bang echoed over the rooftops,
and Karlson shouted:

'Open up, it's the police!'

In their attic, Rollo and Spike flew up from the
floor as if their trousers were on fire.

'Runno, roll for it,' yelled Spike.

He meant 'Rollo, run for it,' but when Spike was
scared, he got his words all mixed up.

'Quick, into the drawerwobe,' he yelled, and the
pair of them went crashing into the wardrobe, slam-
ming the door shut after them, so they could no

longer be seen. But Spike could be heard, anxiously calling from inside:

'Rike and Spollo are not at home I tell you! No, they're *not* at home, they've gone out!'

Afterwards, when Karlson and Smidge were back on their porch steps, Smidge hung his head dejectedly. He knew now what a hard job lay ahead of him, trying to keep an eye on Karlson, who was so reckless, what with types like Spike and Rollo living just round the corner. And on top of all that, Miss Crawley and Uncle Julius . . . Oh dear, he'd forgotten to tell Karlson about them!

'Listen, Karlson . . . ' he began. But Karlson wasn't listening. He had started on the next stage of the bun feast, and was busy glugging squash from a little blue mug that had once been Smidge's and that Smidge had given him on his last birthday, three months ago. He was holding the mug firmly with both hands, like little children do, but then oops! he dropped it anyway, like little children always do.

'Oh no,' cried Smidge, because it was a nice little blue mug and it would be a shame if it broke. But luckily it didn't. As it went tumbling down over Karlson's feet, he cleverly caught it between his two big toes. He had taken off his shoes, you see, and his big toes were sticking out of the holes in his red and white stripy socks like two little black sausages.

'The world's best big toes, guess who's got them,' said Karlson.

He looked lovingly at the two little black sausages and kept himself amused for quite a while, curling and uncurling his toes to make the big ones poke in and out of the holes in his socks.

'Listen, Karlson . . . ' Smidge tried again, but Karlson interrupted him.

'You can do sums,' he said. 'If the whole of me is worth ten thousand kronor, how many five öre pieces do you think I can get for my big toes?'

Smidge laughed.

'I don't know. Are you thinking of selling them?'

'Yes,' said Karlson. 'To you. You'll get them pretty cheap, because they're a bit second-hand. And . . . ' he went on, considering the matter, 'um . . . a bit grubby.'

'Are you crazy?' said Smidge. 'You can't manage without big toes, can you?'

'Did I say I could?' demanded Karlson. 'They'll stay put on my feet, but they'll *belong* to you. I'll just be borrowing them.'

He put his feet on Smidge's lap so Smidge could see that they were virtually his already, and said encouragingly:

'Just think, every time you see them you'll be able to say: "Those sweet little big toes are mine!" Won't that be lovely?'

But Smidge didn't want to buy any big toes. He promised to give Karlson some five öre pieces anyway, since he had some in his piggy bank. And then, at last, he could say what needed saying.

'Listen, Karlson,' he said, 'guess who's coming to look after me while Mum and Dad go off on holiday?'

'The world's best child-looker-after, I expect,' said Karlson.

'Do you mean you?' asked Smidge, though he knew very well that it was exactly what Karlson meant. And Karlson nodded in agreement.

'Yep, if you can show me a better child-looker-after, I'll give you five öre.'

'Miss Crawley,' said Smidge. He was afraid Karlson would be angry because Mum had asked Miss Crawley to come, when the world's best child-looker-after was to hand, just up there on the roof, but strangely enough Karlson seemed delighted and in the best of moods.

'Whoop, whoop,' was all he would say. 'Whoop, whoop.'

'What do you mean, whoop, whoop?' asked Smidge uneasily.

'When I say whoop, whoop, I mean whoop, whoop,' declared Karlson, looking at Smidge with a glint in his eyes.

'And Uncle Julius is coming, too,' said Smidge. 'He's got to go to the doctor for several lots of treatment because he's so stiff all over in the mornings.'

And he told Karlson all about how difficult Uncle Julius was, and how he would be staying at the flat the whole time Mum and Dad were cruising around on the white steamer and Seb and Sally were both away.

'I wonder how it's going to turn out,' said Smidge anxiously.

'Whoop,' said Karlson, 'they'll get a couple of weeks they'll never forget.'

'Do you mean Mum and Dad or Seb and Sally?' wondered Smidge.

'I mean Creepy Crawley and Uncle Julius,' said Karlson.

That made Smidge even more worried. But Karlson gave him a comforting pat on the cheek.

'Easy now, take it easy! We'll play some nice games with them, because we're the kindest in the world . . . at least I am.'

And he fired off a shot, right by Smidge's ear, making Smidge jump out of his skin with fright.

'And poor Uncle Julius won't need to go to the doctor for his treatment,' said Karlson. 'I'll deal with all that.'

'How?' asked Smidge. 'Surely you don't know what sort of treatment you have to give a person who's stiff all over?'

'Don't I?' said Karlson. 'I promise you I shall have Uncle Julius as swift and nimble as a greyhound . . . There are three ways.'

'Which three?' asked Smidge suspiciously.

'Tirritation, jiggery-pokery, and figuration,' said Karlson. 'He won't need any treatment apart from those.'

Smidge was looking round anxiously, because people were starting to stick their heads out of windows on all sides, to see who had fired a shot, and then he noticed Karlson was reloading the pistol.

'No, Karlson,' said Smidge, 'please, Karlson, don't shoot any more!'

'Easy now, take it easy!' said Karlson. 'You know what,' he went on, 'I'm just having an idea. Do you reckon Creepy Crawley might be a bit stiff as well?'

Before Smidge could reply, Karlson raised the pistol with a cheer, and fired. It went off with a huge bang that echoed over the rooftops. From all the houses around came the sound of voices, alarmed and angry, and one of them shouted something about calling the police. Smidge was beside himself. Karlson just sat there, calmly munching the last of the buns.

'What are you making such a fuss about?' he asked Smidge. 'Don't they know it's my birthday?'

He swallowed the last mouthful of bun. And then he burst into song, a happy little song that rang out wonderfully into the summer evening.

It's got to go bang and I've got to have fun
With a tralala and a tumty tum
And what is a birthday without a bun?
With a tralala and a tumty tum.
It's got to be heysan and hopsan and hi,
And everyone's s'posed to be nice as pie
With a whoop-de-whoop
And a loop the loop
And a tumty tumty tum.

KARLSON IS THE BEST IN THE CLASS

The evening Mum and Dad set off for the start of their cruise, it was pouring. The rain was lashing the window panes and roaring down the drainpipes from the roof. Ten minutes before they were due to leave, Miss Crawley came bustling through the front door, as drenched as a drowned cat and as peevish as an old pirate.

'At last,' said Mum. 'At last!'

She had been waiting all day, and now she was feeling nervous, but Miss Crawley didn't appreciate that. She said grumpily:

'I couldn't come any sooner. It was Frida's fault.'

There was so much Mum needed to tell Miss Crawley, but now there was no time, because the taxi was already waiting outside.

'The most important thing is this little boy of ours,' said Mum, the tears welling up in her eyes. 'Oh I do hope nothing will happen to him while we're gone.'

'Nothing happens where I am,' Miss Crawley assured them, and Dad said he could well understand that. He was sure everything would be fine, he said, and then Mum and Dad hugged Smidge goodbye, dashed out of the door and disappeared into the lift . . . and Smidge was left alone with Miss Crawley.

She sat at the kitchen table, big and beefy and peevish, smoothing back her wet hair with her big, beefy hands. Smidge looked at her shyly and gave her a little smile, to be welcoming. He remembered the last time they had had her in the house, and how scared he had been of her then, and how much he had disliked her to start with. But it wasn't like that any more, in fact it was almost a comfort to have her there. And even though things were likely to get very complicated with her and Karlson in the same house, Smidge was still grateful to Miss Crawley for coming. Mum would never ever have let him stay at home and keep an eye on Karlson otherwise, he was sure of that. So Smidge wanted to show he was friends with Miss Crawley right from the start, and he asked politely:

'How's Frida?'

Miss Crawley didn't answer; she merely gave a sniff. Frida was Miss Crawley's sister. Smidge had never met her, only heard about her. And he had heard a great deal about her. From Miss Crawley. Miss Crawley lived with Frida in a flat on Frey Street, but they didn't seem to enjoy each other's company much. Smidge had realized Miss Crawley had it in for her sister and thought she was snooty and always putting on airs. It had all started when Frida had been on a television programme about ghosts, which had annoyed Miss Crawley a lot. Admittedly she had later featured in a television programme herself, showing the whole of Sweden how to cook Hilda Crawley's Spicy Special, but that obviously hadn't been enough to put Frida in her place. Perhaps she was still being snooty and putting on airs, since Miss Crawley merely sniffed when Smidge asked how Frida was.

'She seems fine, thank you,' said Miss Crawley when she had finished snorting. 'She's got herself a fiancé, poor creature!'

Smidge didn't really know what to say next, but he had to say something and he wanted to be polite, so he asked:

'Have you got a fiancé, Miss Crawley?'

He clearly shouldn't have said that, because Miss Crawley leapt to her feet and started making a great commotion of the washing up.

'No, thank goodness,' she said. 'And I don't want one, either. There's no need for everyone to be as daft as Frida.'

She said no more but attacked the dishes so wildly that the suds went flying everywhere. Then another thought must have occurred to her, because she turned anxiously to Smidge.

'Listen, that horrible, fat little boy you were always playing with last time doesn't come round here any more, I hope?'

Miss Crawley had never understood that Karlson on the Roof was a handsome, thoroughly clever, perfectly plump man in his prime. She thought he was one of Smidge's schoolfriends, the same age as him, and a proper little hooligan. She didn't stop to think too much about the fact that he was a little hooligan who could fly. She thought his motor was something you could buy in any old toyshop, if you had enough money, and she would get worked up about how spoilt children were these days, with all their expensive gadgets. 'I suppose we'll soon have them flying to the moon before they even start school,' she said. And now here she was, calling Karlson 'that horrible, fat little boy'—Smidge thought that was very unkind of her.

'Karlson isn't horrible . . . ' he started, but just then there was a ring at the front door.

'Oh, is that Uncle Julius already?' said Smidge, and ran to open the door.

But it wasn't Uncle Julius; it was Karlson. A thoroughly soaked Karlson, standing there in a little puddle of rainwater with a reproachful look on his face.

'How long am I supposed to fly around in the

pouring rain, cursing because you haven't bothered to leave your window open?' demanded Karlson.

'But you said you were going home to bed,' Smidge defended himself, because Karlson had indeed said just that. 'I honestly didn't think you'd be coming this evening.'

'You could have hoped I might,' said Karlson. 'You could have thought: maybe he'll turn up anyway, dear little Karlson, oh what fun, yes, I expect he will come, because he's bound to want to see Creepy Crawley, you could have thought.'

'And do you want to?' asked Smidge anxiously.

'Whoop, whoop,' said Karlson, his eyes sparkling, 'whoop, whoop, what do *you* think?'

Now Smidge realized very well that he wouldn't be able to keep Karlson and Miss Crawley apart for ever, but he wasn't ready for a confrontation the very first evening. He decided to have a word with Karlson, but Karlson was already on his way to the kitchen, as keen as a dog following a scent. Smidge rushed after him and grabbed his arm.

'You know what, Karlson,' he said encouragingly, 'she thinks you're one of my schoolfriends, and I reckon we should let her carry on thinking that.'

Karlson stopped short. Then he gave an almighty chuckle, the way he always did when something really tickled him.

'Does she really think I go to school?' he said triumphantly. He headed for the kitchen even faster.

Miss Crawley heard galloping footsteps approaching. She was expecting Uncle Julius and was surprised that an elderly man could go so fast. She looked up, ready to see this sprinter in action, but when the door opened and Karlson rushed in, she gave a gasp as if she had seen a snake. A snake that she most definitely did not want in her kitchen.

But that was lost on Karlson. With a couple of bounds he was right in front of her, looking eagerly up into her disapproving face.

'And who do you think is the best in the class?' he asked. 'Guess who's best at reading and writing and sums and ev—everything.'

'People usually say hello when they arrive,' said

Miss Crawley, 'and it's of no interest to me who's the best in the class. It won't be you, anyway.'

'Well it is, so there,' said Karlson, but then he stopped, as if he was thinking. 'Well, I'm best at sums, anyway,' he said gloomily, when he'd finished thinking. But then he shrugged.

'Anyway, that's a mere trifle,' he said, and began cheerily jumping round the kitchen. Round and round Miss Crawley he went, and suddenly he started singing a familiar, merry song:

It's got to go bang and I've got to have fun . . .

'No, Karlson,' said Smidge hastily, 'no, no!'
But it was no use.

With a tralala and a tumty tum . . .

sang Karlson. And when he got to *tumty tum*, there was a sudden bang, followed by a scream. The bang was from Karlson's pistol and the scream was from Miss Crawley. Smidge thought at first she was going to faint, because she sank down on a chair and sat there without a word, eyes closed, but when Karlson went on with his *tralala* and *tumty tum*, she opened her eyes and said angrily:

'I'll give you such a tralala and tumty tum that you'll never forget it, you little brat, if you ever try that again!'

Karlson didn't think that needed any answer. Instead, he jabbed his podgy finger under Miss Crawley's chin at a pretty brooch she was wearing.

'That's very nice,' he said. 'Where did you pinch it from?'

'No, Karlson,' said Smidge, horrified, because he could see how furious Miss Crawley was.

'That . . . that . . . that's the most outrageous thing I've ever heard,' she spluttered, hardly able to get the words out. But then she yelled:

'Get out! Out, I say!'

Karlson looked at her in surprise.

'Now don't take on so,' he said. 'I was only asking. And when a person asks politely, they deserve a polite answer, I think.'

'Out!' shouted Miss Crawley.

'By the way,' said Karlson, 'there's one other thing I'd like to know. Are you a bit stiff in the mornings, too, and if so, how early would you like me to start figurating you?'

Miss Crawley looked around wildly for some weapon she could use to drive Karlson out, and Karlson ran helpfully over to the broom cupboard and pulled out a carpet beater, which he thrust into her hand.

'Whoop, whoop,' he yelled, setting off at the double round the kitchen. 'Whoop, whoop, here we go again!'

But then Miss Crawley threw down the carpet beater. She no doubt remembered what had happened the last time she chased Karlson with a carpet beater, and she didn't want to go through that again.

Smidge could see things had got off to a bad start, and he wondered how long Miss Crawley could stand Karlson darting round the room going whoop, whoop before she went off her head. Not much longer, thought Smidge. The vital thing now was to get Karlson out of the kitchen right away. And as Karlson went sprinting by on his eleventh lap, Smidge grabbed him by the collar.

'Karlson,' he said imploringly, 'let's go into my room instead.'

And Karlson did come with him, but very reluctantly.

'It was daft to stop, though, just when I was getting her going,' he said. 'If I'd had a bit longer, she'd have come steaming after me, as playful as a sealion, I'm sure of it.'

As usual, he went over and poked the peach stone out of the flowerpot to see how much it had grown. Smidge came over to look too, and standing there beside Karlson with his arm round his shoulders, he realized how wet Karlson was, poor thing. He must have been flying round in the rain for ages.

'Isn't it making you freezing cold, being so wet?' asked Smidge.

Karlson didn't seem to have thought about it until now, but he stopped to consider it.

'Yes, of course I'm freezing cold,' he said. 'But who cares, eh? Is anybody sorry to see his best friend arrive soaking wet and shivering with cold, and does he make sure his friend takes off his clothes and hang them up to dry and wrap him in a nice, soft dressing gown and make him some hot chocolate and give him lots of buns to go with it and tuck him up in bed and sing him a lovely, sad song to help him fall into a gentle doze, does he, eh?' He gave Smidge an accusing look.

'No, he doesn't,' went on Karlson, his voice quavering as if he was about to cry.

Hearing this, Smidge lost no time in doing everything Karlson thought you ought to do for your best friend. The hardest part was persuading Miss Crawley to agree to let Karlson have the hot chocolate and buns, but she had neither the time nor the energy to object for long, because she was busy roasting a chicken ready for Uncle Julius, who was expected very soon.

'You'll have to see to it as best you can,' she said. So that was what Smidge did. Then Karlson, round and rosy, sat in Smidge's bed, wearing Smidge's white dressing gown, and had his hot chocolate and buns while his shirt and trousers and underwear and shoes and socks hung in the bathroom to dry.

'You needn't bother with the sad song,' said Karlson, 'but you can start trying to talk me into staying the night.'

'Oh, do you want to?' asked Smidge.

Karlson was just stuffing a whole bun into his mouth, so he couldn't answer, but he nodded

vigorously. Bumble barked. He didn't think Karlson should be in Smidge's bed. But Smidge gathered Bumble into his arms and whispered in his ear:

'I can sleep on my sofa, see, and we can move your basket over there, too!'

Miss Crawley clattered something in the kitchen, and when Karlson heard her he said indignantly:

'She didn't believe I was the best in the class!'

'That was hardly surprising,' said Smidge. He knew very well that Karlson wasn't much good at reading or writing or sums—worst of all at sums, although he had told Miss Crawley just the opposite.

'You should do a bit of practice,' said Smidge. 'Would you like me to teach you some addition, mm?'

Karlson gave such a snort that his hot chocolate sprayed all over the place.

'And would you like me to teach you some manners, mm? Do you think I don't know all about addi . . . er . . . what you said?'

There was no time for practising sums, anyway, because just then they heard a loud ring at the front door. Smidge knew it really must be Uncle Julius this time, and dashed to let him in. He really wanted to be on his own to meet Uncle Julius, and he thought Karlson would stay in bed. But Karlson thought differently. He came scurrying after Smidge with the dressing gown flapping round his ankles.

Smidge opened the front door wide, and sure enough, there stood Uncle Julius with a suitcase in each hand.

'Welcome, Uncle Jul—' began Smidge. That was as far as he got, because just then there was a terrific bang, and the next moment Uncle Julius collapsed onto the floor in a faint.

'Oh, Karlson, no!' said Smidge despairingly. How sorry he was that he had ever given Karlson that pistol. 'Whatever are we going to do now? Why did you have to do that?'

'You need a gun salute,' claimed Karlson. 'In fact, you *have* to have a gun salute when posh, professional people come to visit.'

Smidge was so shaken he was on the verge of tears. Bumble was barking wildly and Miss Crawley, who had also heard the shot, came running, all out of breath, and started flapping her arms and wailing about poor Uncle Julius, who lay there on the doormat like a felled pine tree in the forest. Karlson was the only one who took it all calmly.

'Easy now, take it easy,' he said.

He snatched up the watering can Smidge's mum used for her houseplants, and gave Uncle Julius a generous shower of water. And it worked: Uncle Julius slowly opened his eyes.

'It just keeps on raining,' he mumbled. But when he saw all the worried faces gathered round him, he woke up properly.

'Wh . . . wh . . . what's going on?' he roared crossly.

'A salute,' said Karlson, 'that's what's going on,

but it's totally wasted on some people, when all they do is faint like that.'

Miss Crawley took charge of Uncle Julius. She dried him off and led him to the main bedroom, which he was going to use during his visit, and they could hear her telling him that the horrid, fat little boy was one of Smidge's schoolfriends, who needed kicking out whenever he showed his face.

'Hear that,' said Smidge to Karlson. 'You've got to promise: no more salutes!'

'Oh, all right,' said Karlson sulkily. 'You do your best to make things nice and special for the guests, but does anybody rush up and kiss you on both cheeks and tell you you're the world's best jester? Not on your life! Snobs and spoilsports, the lot of you!'

Smidge wasn't paying any attention. He was listening to Uncle Julius's complaints from the bedroom. The mattress was too hard, Uncle Julius said, and the bed was too short and the covers were too thin. Oh yes, there was no mistaking that Uncle Julius had arrived.

'He's never satisfied with anything,' Smidge said

to Karlson. 'The only thing he's perfectly satisfied with is himself, I reckon.'

'I can soon get him out of that habit, if you ask me nicely,' said Karlson.

But Smidge asked Karlson nicely to do no such thing.

KARLSON STAYS THE NIGHT

A little while later, Uncle Julius was sitting at the table eating his chicken, while Miss Crawley and Smidge and Karlson and Bumble stood in a row, watching him. Just like a king, thought Smidge. His teacher at school had told them that kings long ago always used to have people to stand and watch while they ate.

Uncle Julius was fat, and looked very stuck up and pleased with himself, but those old kings used to look like that, too, sometimes, Smidge remembered.

'Take that dog out,' said Uncle Julius. 'You know I don't like dogs, Smidge.'

'But Bumble isn't doing anything,' objected Smidge. 'He's being very good and quiet.'

Then Uncle Julius put on that jokey face he always used when he was about to say something unpleasant.

'I see, that's how it is these days,' he said. 'Little boys answer back when they get told off, do they? I can't say I like it very much.'

Karlson hadn't been able to take his eyes off the chicken, but now he looked thoughtfully at Uncle Julius. He stood for a long while, gazing at him.

'Uncle Julius,' he said in the end, 'has anyone ever told you that you are a handsome, thoroughly clever, perfectly plump man in your prime?'

Uncle Julius certainly hadn't been expecting such a fine compliment. He was flattered, you could see that, even if he tried not to show it. He just gave a modest little laugh and said:

'No, no one's ever told me that!'

'Oh, haven't they?' asked Karlson. 'Well, how did you get such a ridiculous idea into your skull, then?'

'Karlson, no . . . ' said Smidge reproachfully, because he really did think Karlson had gone too far. But that made Karlson lose his temper.

'Karlson, no, and Karlson, no, and Karlson, no,' he said. 'Why do you have to go on like that all the time? I haven't done anything!'

Uncle Julius gave Karlson a stern look, but then seemed to decide to ignore him altogether. He went on with his chicken, and Miss Crawley tried to persuade him to have a bit more.

'I hope you like it,' she said.

Uncle Julius sank his teeth into his chicken with a crunch of bone, and said in that jokey way of his:

'Why yes, thanks! But this chicken must be at least four or five years old, I can tell by the teeth.'

Miss Crawley gave a gasp and two angry frown lines appeared on her forehead.

'But chickens don't have teeth,' she declared sharply.

That made Uncle Julius put on an even more comical expression.

'No, but I do,' he said.

'Though not at nights, or so I've heard,' said

Karlson, and Smidge flushed bright red, because he was the one who had told Karlson that Uncle Julius kept his teeth in a glass of water beside the bed when he was asleep.

Luckily, at that moment Miss Crawley began to howl because Uncle Julius thought the chicken was tough. If there was one thing she was sensitive about it was people criticizing her cooking, and now she was crying bitterly.

Uncle Julius definitely hadn't expected her to take it so badly. He quickly thanked her for the meal and looked almost shamefaced as he went over to the rocking chair, where he found a newspaper to hide behind.

Karlson glowered angrily at him.

'Goodness me, some people can be mean,' he said, and dashed over to start patting Miss Crawley wherever he could reach.

'There there, sweetie,' he said consolingly. 'Tough chickens, they're a mere trifle, you know, and you can't help it that you've never been able to cook.'

But that made Miss Crawley let out a terrific yell, and she gave Karlson such a wallop that he found himself flying backwards across the room to end up in the rocking chair, on Uncle Julius's lap.

'Whoop, whoop,' screeched Karlson in a shrill voice, and before Uncle Julius had time to shake him off, Karlson had made himself comfortable there. He pulled his toes up under the dressing gown and curled himself into a soft little ball and said with a contented purr:

'Shall we play that you're my grandpa and you tell me a story, but it mustn't be too scary, because then I get so frightened.'

Uncle Julius didn't want to be Karlson's grandpa in the least, and besides, he had found something interesting in the paper. He bundled Karlson onto the floor without further ado and turned to Miss Crawley.

'What's this in the paper?' he asked. 'Have you got spies here in Vasa?'

Smidge was scared stiff when he heard that. Now they were in a fix! Why did Uncle Julius have to get his hands on that wretched paper? After all, it was over a week old now, and should have been thrown out long ago.

But luckily, Uncle Julius just jeered at the sorts of things they wrote in the newspaper.

'They think they can make us swallow any old nonsense,' he said. 'And they'll write absolutely anything, just to get people to buy copies. Spy . . . how stupid can you get! I hardly imagine you've seen a spyplane or UFO flying around these parts, Miss Crawley?'

Smidge held his breath. If she tells him that the horrid, fat boy can fly, then the game's up, he thought, because that will make Uncle Julius start to think.

But Miss Crawley clearly couldn't get it into her head that there was anything strange about Karlson's flying, and anyway, she was still sobbing so much she could hardly speak.

'Spies, no, none that I've seen,' she said through her sobs. 'That's just the sort of rubbish the papers write, isn't it.'

Smidge gave a sigh of relief. If only he could persuade Karlson never, ever to fly when Uncle Julius might see him, perhaps everything would be all right after all.

Smidge looked round for Karlson, but there was no sign of him. Karlson had vanished. That worried Smidge and he wanted to go and look for him straight away, but Uncle Julius kept him talking. He had to know how Smidge was getting on at school and test him on his mental arithmetic, although it was the summer holidays and everything. Finally Smidge managed to get away, and ran to his room to check if Karlson was there.

'Karlson,' he called as he came through the door. 'Karlson, where are you?'

'In your pyjama trousers,' said Karlson. 'If these useless sausage skins can be called pyjama trousers!'

He was sitting on the edge of the bed, trying to squeeze himself into Smidge's pyjama bottoms, but however much he struggled, he couldn't do it.

'I'll get you some of Seb's pyjamas,' said Smidge, and ran to get a pair from Seb's room, in a size that had some chance of fitting a perfectly plump man like Karlson. The trouser legs and sleeves were much too long, of course, but Karlson soon sorted that out by chopping them off. Smidge didn't notice in time, but when he did he decided not to let it worry him.

Pyjamas were a mere trifle and mustn't be allowed to ruin the fun of having Karlson staying the night.

Smidge had made up a bed for himself with Seb's bedcovers on the sofa, and had put Bumble's basket beside it. Bumble was lying in it, trying to sleep, but every now and then he would open one eye and take a suspicious peep at Karlson.

Karlson was squirming around in Smidge's bed, getting comfortable.

'I want it to be like a warm little nest,' he said.

He looked really sweet in Seb's blue and white striped pyjamas, Smidge thought, and if he would just let Smidge tuck him in properly, then it really would be like a warm little nest.

But Karlson didn't want to be tucked in.

'Not yet,' he said. 'There are lots of exciting things you're supposed to do when you spend the night at someone else's. You're supposed to eat salami sandwiches in bed and then make an apple-pie bed and have a pillow fight. We'll start with the salami sandwiches.'

'But you've just had a whole lot of buns,' said Smidge.

'If we're not going to do what you're *supposed* to do, you can count me out,' said Karlson. 'Get the sandwiches!'

So Smidge crept into the kitchen and made some sandwiches. There was nobody to disturb him. Miss Crawley was in the sitting room, talking to Uncle Julius. She must have forgiven him for what he said about the chicken.

Then Smidge perched on the edge of the bed and watched Karlson munching sandwiches. He felt very happy: it was such good fun having his best friend to stay, and even Karlson seemed pleased and satisfied for once.

'Sandwiches are great and you're great and Creepy Crawley's great, too,' he said. 'Though she didn't believe I was the best in the class,' he added, and his face clouded over. You could see he was still fretting about it.

'Oh, I wouldn't worry!' said Smidge. 'Uncle Julius wants me to be the best in the class, and I'm not.'

'I should say not,' said Karlson. 'But I could teach you a bit of addi—what you said.'

'Addition,' said Smidge. 'You think *you* can teach *me*?'

'Yes, because I'm the world's best additionater.'

Smidge laughed.

'All right, we'll give it a try,' he said. 'Can I count you in?'

Karlson nodded.

'Fire away!'

So Smidge began.

'Let's say Mum gives you three apples . . . '

'Yes please, I'll have them now,' said Karlson.

'Don't interrupt,' said Smidge. 'Say you get three apples from Mum and two from Dad and two from Seb and three from Sally and one from me . . . '

He got no further before Karlson held up an accusing finger.

'I knew it,' said Karlson. 'I knew you were the meanest in this family, and that's saying something, in this place.'

'Sshh, we're not talking about that now,' said Smidge, but Karlson went stubbornly on:

'It would have been nice if you'd packed me up

plenty of apples and a couple of pears and a few of those yummy little yellow plums, you know the kind!'

'Don't make things awkward, Karlson,' said Smidge. 'This is only addition . . . you get one apple from Mum . . . '

'Stop!' yelled Karlson angrily. 'I'm not standing for that. What's she done with the other two I was getting from her just now?'

Smidge sighed.

'Karlson, please, the apples don't matter. I'm only using them to help you understand what this is all about.'

Karlson gave a snort.

'Oh, I understand what it's all about. It's all about your mum gobbling up my apples as soon as I take my eyes off her.'

'Don't make things awkward, Karlson,' Smidge said again. 'If you get three apples from Mum . . . '

Karlson nodded approvingly.

'See! It helps to speak up for yourself! I knew it. Just try to keep tabs on all this now! I'm to have three apples from your mum and two from your dad and two from Seb and three from Sally and one from you, because you're the meanest . . .'

'Yes, how many apples will you have then?' asked Smidge.

'What do you think?' said Karlson.

'I don't think, because I know,' declared Smidge.

'Tell me, then,' said Karlson.

'No, it's you who has to tell *me*, you know that.'

'Don't go getting ideas! You tell me, and I bet you get it wrong!'

'Well I won't, so there,' said Smidge. 'You'll have eleven apples.'

'That's what you think,' said Karlson. 'But you're wide of the mark there, because I pinched twenty-six apples from a garden out at Lidingö the night before last, and I've still got three left, plus one I've only taken a few bites of—so what do you say to that, eh?'

Smidge didn't know what to say at first. But then he had a flash of inspiration.

'Hah, I know you're lying,' he said, 'because there are no apples on the trees in June.'

'Is that so?' said Karlson. 'Well, where did you and

all the other apple thieves in this house get yours from, then?'

That was when Smidge gave up trying to teach Karlson to do sums.

'But at least you know what addition is now,' he said.

'You think I haven't realized it's the same as scrumping apples?' said Karlson. 'And you don't need to teach me that, because I can do it already. I'm the world's best apple additionater, and if I can just find time, I'll take you out to Lidingö and show you how it's done.'

Karlson crammed the last bit of sandwich into his mouth, and started on the pillow fight. But it didn't go very well, because Bumble started barking frantically as soon as Karlson thumped Smidge round the head with the pillow.

'Woof,' went Bumble, and grabbed the pillow between his teeth, and they each stood there tugging, Bumble and Karlson, until the pillow burst. Then Karlson threw it up to the ceiling and all the feathers came flying out and sailed gracefully down onto Smidge, who was lying on the sofa, laughing his head off.

'I think it's snowing,' said Karlson. 'It's snowing harder and harder,' he said, and hurled the pillow into the air again. But then Smidge said that had better be the end of the pillow fight, and anyway, it was time to get to sleep. It was getting late, and they could hear Uncle Julius saying goodnight to Miss Crawley out in the hall.

'I shall take myself off to my short bed,' said Uncle Julius.

Karlson suddenly looked remarkably cheerful.

'Whoop, whoop,' he said. 'I'm sitting here looking forward to a bit of fun.'

'What sort of fun?' asked Smidge.

'The sort of fun you're supposed to have when you stay the night at someone's,' said Karlson.

'Making an apple-pie bed, you mean? But it's too late for that now—you can't do that.'

'You're right, it's too late now,' said Karlson.

'Yes, it is,' said Smidge, relieved.

'So I can't do that,' declared Karlson.

'Good,' said Smidge.

'Because I've already done it,' said Karlson.

Smidge sat up in his sofa bed in surprise.

'Who to? Surely not Uncle Julius?'

Karlson gave a hearty chuckle.

'Clever boy, *however* did you guess?'

Smidge had got so carried away with laughing during the pillow fight that he gave a giggle, even though he knew he shouldn't.

'Oh dear, that's going to make Uncle Julius very cross,' he said.

'Yes, that's what I need to check up on,' said Karlson. 'So I'm thinking of taking a little flight and peeping through the bedroom window.'

That made Smidge stop giggling.

'Not on your life! What if he spots you? He'll think you're that spy, and you know what'll happen next.'

But Karlson wouldn't be talked out of it. If you had made an apple-pie bed, you had to see how cross the person you'd made it for was, otherwise there was no point, he declared.

'And anyway, I can hide under the umbrella.'

He had brought Mum's red umbrella from beside the front door, because it was still pouring with rain.

'I don't want to get Seb's pyjamas wet, do I now?' said Karlson.

He stood at the window holding the open umbrella over his head, ready for take off. It was awfully risky, thought Smidge, and he begged Karlson:

'Be careful, whatever you do! Be careful not to let him see you, otherwise we've had it!'

'Easy now, take it easy,' said Karlson. And out he flew, into the rain.

Smidge was left there feeling not in the least like taking it easy. In fact he was so nervous that he couldn't help biting his knuckles.

The minutes passed, the rain fell, and Smidge waited. Then suddenly he heard Uncle Julius give a piercing cry for help from the bedroom. A moment later, Karlson came flying in through the window. Chortling with glee, he switched off his motor and propped the umbrella on the rug to dry.

'Did he see you?' Smidge asked him anxiously. 'Is he in bed yet?'

'He's trying to be,' said Karlson.

There were more loud cries from Uncle Julius.

'I'll have to go and see what's the matter,' said Smidge, and dashed to the bedroom.

There sat Uncle Julius, all tangled up in his sheets, white in the face, his eyes wide with shock, and on the floor beside him was a big muddle of blankets and pillows.

'I don't want to talk to you!' said Uncle Julius when he saw Smidge. 'Fetch Miss Crawley!'

But Miss Crawley must have heard his cries, too, for she came loping along from the kitchen, and stopped stock still in the doorway.

'Lordy lordy,' she said. 'Are you remaking your bed, Mr Janson?'

'No I am not,' said Uncle Julius, 'though I must say I don't like the new way of making beds that you go in for in this house . . . But I can't be bothered with that now.'

He stopped and gave a little moan, which made Miss Crawley stride across the room and put her hand on his brow.

'What's the matter, Mr Janson, are you feeling ill?'

'Yes, I'm ill,' said Uncle Julius heavily. 'I *must* be ill . . . You make yourself scarce,' he added to Smidge.

And Smidge did. But he stopped outside the door, because he very much wanted to hear the rest of the story.

'I am a sober and sensible man,' said Uncle Julius. 'Neither the newspapers nor anybody else can make me believe idiotic things . . . So I must be ill.'

'How do you mean?' asked Miss Crawley.

'It's these visions . . . these feverish visions,' said Uncle Julius. And then he lowered his voice so far that Smidge could hardly hear him.

'I don't want you to tell this to a soul,' whispered Uncle Julius, 'but the fact is: I've seen the Sandman.'

KARLSON DOES SOME TASTY TIRRITATION

When Smidge woke up the next morning, Karlson had disappeared. Seb's pyjamas were in a heap on the floor and the window was open, so Smidge knew he must have flown back home. It felt empty, but in some ways it was just as well. Now Miss Crawley wouldn't have anything to make a fuss about. She didn't even need to know Karlson had stayed the night at Smidge's. But it was still strange how quiet and dull and sort of grey everything went as soon as Karlson wasn't there. However difficult it was to keep him in order, Smidge still always missed him when they were apart, and he decided he simply must send Karlson a message.

So he went and tugged three times on the string that was cleverly hidden behind the curtain. It was part of a bell system Karlson had rigged up so Smidge would be able to send him signals. If you pulled the string, a bell rang up at Karlson's, and Karlson had decided what different rings would mean. If you ring once, it means 'Come straight away', Karlson had said. Twice means 'Don't come whatever you do', and three times means 'Just imagine there being somebody in the world as handsome and perfectly plump and brave and great in every way as you, Karlson.' It was this last message that Smidge wanted to send Karlson. So he yanked the string three times, and heard the bell pealing up on the roof. And goodness, he got an answer, too! A loud pistol shot rang out from the roof, and although it sounded very faint and distant, he could make out Karlson singing his *With a tralala and a tumty tum*.

'Oh, Karlson, no,' whispered Smidge. Stupid Karlson, he was out and about up there, firing his pistol and bawling his head off! How easy it would be for Rollo or Spike or somebody else to hear him and see him and catch him, and sell him to the newspaper for ten thousand kronor!

'But he's only got himself to blame,' said Smidge to Bumble, who was lying there in his basket, looking as if he understood everything. Smidge put on his shirt and trousers and then he played with Bumble for a bit, while he waited for the household to come to life.

Uncle Julius couldn't be awake yet, or at least there was no sound from his bedroom, but the smell of fresh coffee gradually began to drift from the kitchen, and Smidge went along there to see what Miss Crawley was up to.

There she sat, as vast as ever, enjoying her first cup of coffee of the day, and strangely enough she had no objection to Smidge joining her at the table. There was no sign of any porridge, but Miss Crawley had clearly got up early and done some baking.

There were two trays of warm buns on the worktop, smelling lovely, and lots more in the basket she had put on the table. Smidge helped himself to a bun and a glass of milk and then they sat there, he and Miss Crawley, eating and drinking in silence. Until Miss Crawley said:

'I wonder how Frida's getting on at home!'

Smidge regarded her thoughtfully over his glass of milk. What if Miss Crawley missed Frida as much as he missed Karlson when they were apart?

'Are you missing Frida, Miss Crawley?' he asked kindly.

Miss Crawley gave a grim laugh.

'Hah, you obviously don't know Frida!'

Smidge wasn't really interested in Frida. But Miss Crawley seemed to want to talk about her, so he asked:

'Who's Frida engaged to?'

'A villain,' said Miss Crawley with great force. 'Oh yes, I know he's a villain, because I've discovered he's getting money out of her.'

The very thought of it made Miss Crawley gnash her teeth, and then she began pouring out her tale.

She clearly hadn't got many people she could talk to, poor thing, thought Smidge, if even a boy like him would do when she wanted to tell someone about Frida. And she most certainly did want to. Smidge had to sit there and hear all about Frida and her Mike and how daft she'd gone since Mike had kept telling her what lovely eyes she'd got, and what a charmingly homely nose, the sort you could rely on in all weathers, as Mike put it.

'Charming nose?' said Miss Crawley with a snort. 'Well, only if your idea of charming is a medium-sized potato in the middle of somebody's face . . .'

'So what does Mike look like, then?' asked Smidge, to show he was interested.

'I haven't a clue, thank goodness,' said Miss Crawley. 'You needn't think Frida would let me see him.'

Miss Crawley didn't know what sort of job Mike had, either. But he had a friend called Roland, Frida had said.

'And he might have suited me, Frida says, but of course nobody would want me because I'm not nice-looking enough, she says . . . I suppose she means no charming nose or anything like that,' said Miss Crawley, and gave another snort. Then all of a sudden she got up and disappeared out to the hall to fetch something. And the minute she was out of the door, Karlson came flying in at the window.

Smidge was really cross.

'Karlson, not again! You *know* I've asked you not to fly where Miss Crawley or Uncle Julius can see you . . . '

'And I'm not flying where Miss Crawley or Uncle Julius can see me, either,' said Karlson. 'In actual fact, I'm not showing myself one single bit,' he said, and crept under the kitchen table. And there he was sitting, well hidden by the dangling folds of the tablecloth, when Miss Crawley came back with the cardigan she'd gone to fetch.

She poured herself some more coffee and took another bun, and then she went on with her tale.

'As I was saying . . . I've no homely potato nose to boast about.'

Then they heard a voice, one of those funny voices like ventriloquists use, so you don't quite know where they're coming from, and the voice said:

'No, yours is more a sort of cucumber, with knobbly bits.'

Miss Crawley gave a start, making the coffee almost slosh out of her cup, and glared suspiciously at Smidge.

'Are you being cheeky?'

Smidge went red and didn't know what to say.

'N-no,' he stammered, 'I think there's a programme about vegetables on the radio, all about tomatoes and cucumbers and that sort of stuff.'

That was a brainwave, because they could often hear next door's radio in the Stevensons' kitchen, and Miss Crawley had noticed this and complained about it before.

She muttered a bit, but then she had other things to think about, because Uncle Julius came into the kitchen and wanted coffee, too. He hobbled round the table a couple of times, groaning with each step.

'What a night,' he said. 'Ye gods and little fishes, what a night! I was stiff to start with, but that bed and the way those bedclothes were tucked in, oh dear, oh dear!'

He sat down heavily at the table and stared straight ahead as if he was thinking about something in particular. He didn't seem himself, Smidge thought.

'And yet I'm glad, and grateful for last night,' said Uncle Julius finally. 'It's made a new man of me.'

'That's good, because the old one certainly needed replacing.'

It was that funny voice again, and Miss Crawley gave another start and looked suspiciously at Smidge.

'It's the Lindbergs' radio again . . . I think they've turned over to a programme about old cars,' stuttered Smidge.

 Uncle Julius simply didn't notice. He was so absorbed in his thoughts that he neither heard nor saw a thing. Miss Crawley poured him a cup of coffee, and he absent-mindedly put out his hand for a

bun. But he had no sooner picked one up than another hand, a podgy little one, reached up over the edge of the table and grabbed the bun. And Uncle Julius didn't notice. He was lost in thought, and it was only when he dipped his fist in the hot coffee that he came to his senses and realized there was no bun to dunk. He blew on his hand and was a bit annoyed, but then he sank back into his thoughts.

'There are more things between heaven and earth than anyone could dream of, I realized last night,' he said gravely. As he did so, he stretched out a hand and took another bun. And once again a podgy little fist popped up and took the bun. But Uncle Julius didn't notice, he was too deep in thought, and it was only when he put his thumb in his mouth and took a big bite that he came to his senses and realized there was no bun to bite. That made him cross again for a moment, but obviously the new Uncle Julius was nicer than the old one, because he soon calmed down. He didn't even try to take another bun, but just drank his coffee, wrapped up in his thoughts.

The buns were soon all gone, even so. They vanished from the basket one after another, and Smidge was the only one who noticed where they were going. He giggled without making a sound and carefully passed a glass of milk down under the table, so Karlson wouldn't find the buns too dry.

This was what Karlson called 'bun tirritation'! Miss Crawley had found out what it was like to be on the receiving end, last time she was staying with them.

'You can tirritate people tremendously, just by eating up their buns,' Karlson had said. And yes, he knew it was really 'irritate', but 'tirritate' was more fiendish, he claimed.

And now Karlson had embarked on another fiendish bun tirritation, though Miss Crawley hadn't realized yet. Still less Uncle Julius. He wouldn't have noticed a bun tirritation no matter how fiendish it was, because he was so absorbed in thought. But all at once he grasped Miss Crawley's hand and held it hard, as if he wanted to ask for help.

'I must tell somebody about it,' he said. 'I know now, Miss Crawley, that it wasn't a feverish vision. I wasn't delirious, I *saw* the Sandman!'

Miss Crawley's eyes opened wide.

'Can it really be true?'

'Yes,' said Uncle Julius. 'And that's why I am now a new man in a new world. Fairyland, you see, that is what revealed itself to me last night. Because if the Sandman actually exists, why shouldn't there be witches and trolls and ghosts as well, and elves and brownies and all those other mystical beings you read about in fairy stories?'

'And maybe even flying spies,' put in Miss Crawley, trying to suck up to Uncle Julius, but he wasn't having it.

'Stuff and nonsense,' he said. 'I think we can ignore the sort of rubbish they write in the newspapers.'

He leant towards Miss Crawley and looked deep into her eyes.

'Just remember,' he said. 'Our ancestors believed in trolls and brownies and witches and all that. So how can we be so sure those mystical beings don't exist? Do we understand the world better than our ancestors, eh? No, only a blockhead could claim anything so stupid.'

Miss Crawley didn't want to be thought a blockhead. She said there might well be more witches than anybody imagined, and maybe a few trolls and other mystical beings too, for all she knew, if you kept your eyes open and counted properly.

But then Uncle Julius had to stop brooding because he had an appointment with the doctor and it was time to go. Smidge kindly went to see him off at the front door, and so did Miss Crawley. Smidge passed him his walking stick, after Miss Crawley had helped him on with his coat. He seemed quite worn out, poor Uncle Julius, so it was a good thing he was seeing the doctor, thought Smidge, and gave Uncle Julius a shy pat on the hand. Miss Crawley was obviously worried too, because she asked anxiously:

'How are you feeling, Mr Janson? Are you all right?'

'How should I know, until I've seen the doctor,' snapped Uncle Julius.

Well, well, so there *was* some of the old Uncle Julius left, thought Smidge, however much fairyland had been revealed to him.

When Uncle Julius had gone, Smidge and Miss Crawley went back to the kitchen.

'What I'd like now is some more coffee and buns and a bit of peace and quiet,' said Miss Crawley. But then she gave a shriek. There was not a single bun left on the baking trays. In their place was a big paper bag, on which someone had written in terrible, uneven handwriting:

I PINSHED ENUF BUNS FOR ORL MY FERYLAND
FRENDS THE SANT MAN

Miss Crawley read it and frowned grimly.

'No one's going to get me to believe that the Sandman steals buns, assuming he really does exist. He's far too good and noble to do anything like that. No, I know who's done this, all right!'

'Who?' asked Smidge.

'That horrible, fat little boy, of course, Karlson or whatever he's called. Look, the kitchen door's open!

He's been standing out there listening, and he sneaked in when we were in the hall.'

She shook her head angrily.

'The Santman! That's charming, isn't it! Blaming other people, and not even being able to spell!'

Smidge didn't want to get trapped in a discussion about Karlson, so he just said:

'Well, I reckon it was the Sandman, anyway! Come on, Bumble!'

Every morning, Smidge and Bumble went to their local park, and Bumble liked that bit of his day best of all, because there were so many friendly dogs to nose at and talk to.

Smidge usually played with Kris and Jemima, but there was no sign of them today. Maybe they had already gone to the countryside for  their summer holidays, thought Smidge. Oh well, it didn't really matter as long as he had Karlson . . . and Bumble, of course.

A big dog came up and tried to start a fight with Bumble, and Bumble was keen to fight back. He wanted to show that stupid mutt what he thought of him. But Smidge wouldn't let him.

'Don't you dare,' said Smidge. 'You're too small to fight a big dog like that.'

He scooped Bumble up in his arms and looked round for a vacant bench where they could sit until Bumble calmed down. But there were people on all the benches, basking in the summer sunshine, and Smidge had to go right to the far corner of the park to find somewhere to sit. There were already two people sitting  on the bench, two men, each of them clutching a bottle of beer. Two men he recognized! Yes indeed, it was Spike and Rollo. Smidge was scared to start with, and felt like running away. Yet he felt something pulling him towards that bench. He very much wanted to find out if Spike and Rollo were still hunting for Karlson, and this might be one way of finding out. Anyway, what was there to be scared of? After all, Spike and Rollo had never seen him and wouldn't recognize him, luckily. Good, that meant he could sit there beside them for as long as he wanted. That was the sort of thing people did in adventure stories when they wanted to ferret out some information: they sat there quietly, listening for all they were worth.

Smidge sat down on the park bench and pricked up his ears, but he kept chatting to Bumble so Spike and Rollo wouldn't realize he was listening.

It didn't look as though he was going to find out very much. Spike and Rollo just swigged their beer and said nothing. They didn't say a word for a long time. But finally Spike gave a loud belch and said:

'Yeah, we'll have no problem getting our hands on him. We know where he lives, don't we? I've seen him fly in there often enough.'

Smidge was shocked, and so scared he could hardly breathe. Karlson was done for. Spike and Rollo had found his little house on the roof, and that meant the end of everything!

Smidge bit his knuckles and tried not to cry, and he was trying his hardest when he heard Rollo say:

'Yes, I've seen him flying in there more than once, as well . . . It's that flat we were in last summer. Number 12, fourth floor, and the name on the door is Stevenson. I checked.'

Smidge's eyes grew wide with surprise. Had he heard right? Did Spike and Rollo really think Karlson *lived* with the Stevensons? What luck! That must mean Karlson could at any rate hide away and be fairly safe in his own house. Spike and Rollo hadn't found it, thank goodness! But it wasn't altogether surprising. Neither Spike nor Rollo nor anybody else except the chimney sweep ever went wandering around on the roof.

But even though Spike and Rollo hadn't discovered the house, things were bad enough, of course. Poor Karlson, once they started hunting him down in earnest—the silly idiot didn't always have the sense to keep out of the way!

Spike and Rollo had gone quiet again, but then Rollo said in a voice so soft that Smidge could hardly hear it:

'How about tonight?'

Then Spike finally seemed to notice there was

someone else sitting on the bench. He glowered at Smidge and gave a loud cough.

'Yes, maybe tonight's the night to go out and collect a few worms,' he said.

But it wasn't that easy to pull the wool over Smidge's eyes. He knew well enough what Spike and Rollo were planning to do that night. They were planning to catch Karlson while he was asleep in bed, and they thought he would be doing that in the Stevensons' flat.

I must tell Karlson about this, thought Smidge. I must tell him right away!

But Karlson didn't turn up again until just before lunchtime. He wasn't flying this time, but rang the front door bell like other people do. Smidge opened the door.

'Ah, I'm glad you're here . . . ' began Smidge, but Karlson wasn't listening. He hared straight off to see Miss Crawley in the kitchen.

'What sort of spicy special are you making today?' he asked. 'Is it a tough one, or the sort of thing a person with normal fangs can manage?'

Miss Crawley was at the stove making drop

scones so Uncle Julius would have something softer to chew than the chicken, and when she heard Karlson's voice behind her, she gave such a start that she spilt a whole spoonful of batter on the top of the stove. She turned to him, fuming.

'You,' she screeched, 'you . . . you've no shame! You dare to come in here and look me in the face, you horrible little bun thief?'

Karlson covered his face with two pudgy hands and peeked mischievously out through the gap between his fingers.

'Oh yes, I dare, as long as I'm careful,' he said. 'You're not the fairest maiden in all the land, but a person can get used to anything, so I do dare. The main thing is that you should be nice to me . . . give me some drop scones!'

Miss Crawley gave him a furious stare, and then turned to Smidge.

'Listen, did your mother say we were to feed this horrible boy? Is he really supposed to eat here?'

Smidge began to stammer as usual.

'W-well, Mum thinks . . . that Karlson . . . '

'Answer yes or no,' said Miss Crawley, 'did your mother say Karlson was to have his meals here?'

'Well, at any rate, she wants him to—' began Smidge, but Miss Crawley interrupted him in her stoniest voice:

'Answer yes or no, I said! It can't be that hard to answer yes or no to a simple question!'

'So you say,' retorted Karlson. 'I'll ask you a simple question, and then you'll see. Listen! Have you stopped drinking brandy first thing in the morning?'

Miss Crawley gave a gasp and seemed to be about to choke. She tried to speak but couldn't get a word out.

'Come on then, tell us,' said Karlson. 'Have you stopped drinking brandy first thing in the morning?'

'Yes, she has,' said Smidge eagerly. He was really trying to help Miss Crawley, but she blew her top.

'I most certainly have *not*,' she cried in fury, and Smidge was petrified.

'No, no, she *hasn't* stopped,' he corrected himself.

'I'm sorry to hear that,' said Karlson. 'Drunkenness leads to nothing but misery.'

Miss Crawley gave a sort of gurgle and sank down

onto a chair. But Smidge had finally worked out the right answer.

'She hasn't *stopped*, because she never *started*, as you well know,' he told Karlson sternly.

'Did I say she had?' asked Karlson, and turned to Miss Crawley: 'Silly you, now you can see that a yes or no answer won't always work . . . give me some drop scones!'

But if there was one thing in the world Miss Crawley wasn't going to do, it was to give Karlson any drop scones. She ran across the room with a snarl and threw the kitchen door open wide.

'Out,' she yelled. 'Out!'

And Karlson went. He walked haughtily to the door.

'I'm going,' he said. 'I'm glad to go. You're not the only one who can make drop scones!'

Once Karlson was gone, Miss Crawley sat quietly and had a long rest. But then she cast an anxious glance at the clock.

'Whatever can be keeping your Uncle Julius?' she said. 'What if he's got lost? He's not all that used to Stockholm, I don't think.'

Smidge started to worry as well.

'Yes, what if he can't find his way home?'

Just then, the telephone rang in the hall.

'That could be Uncle Julius,' said Smidge, 'ringing to tell us he's lost.'

Miss Crawley went to answer, and Smidge followed her.

But it wasn't Uncle Julius, as Smidge realized when he heard Miss Crawley say in her most peevish voice:

'Oh, it's you, Frida. How are you, still got your nose?'

Smidge didn't want to listen to other people's telephone calls, so he went to his room and settled down to read, but he could still hear a mumble from the hall, and the mumble lasted at least ten minutes.

Smidge was hungry. He wished the mumble would end and Uncle Julius would come home, so they could have lunch at last. Actually, he wanted something to eat right now. And as soon as Miss Crawley hung up, he ran out to the hall to tell her so.

'Oh well, I suppose so,' said Miss Crawley, gruffly obliging, and went ahead of him to the kitchen. But she stopped short at the door. Her beefy form filled the whole doorway, so Smidge couldn't see anything. All he could do was hear her angry shriek, and when he peered inquisitively round her skirt to find out why she was screaming, what he saw was Karlson.

Karlson was sitting at the table, calmly eating drop scones.

Smidge was afraid Miss Crawley was going to kill Karlson, because she looked as if she might. But she just rushed over and grabbed hold of the big plate of drop scones.

'You . . . you . . . you dreadful boy!' she yelled. Then Karlson gave her a little rap over the knuckles.

'Let go of my drop scones,' he said. 'I bought these from the Lindbergs, fair and square for five öre!'

He opened his mouth and stuffed in a huge mouthful.

'As I said—you're not the only one who can make drop scones. All a person has to do is follow his nose, and they turn up all over the place.'

Smidge felt almost sorry for Miss Crawley, because she was totally at a loss.

'Where . . . where . . . where are *my* drop scones, then?' she stuttered, looking over at the stove. There was her serving plate, but it was as empty as empty could be, and seeing that made her furious again.

'Wicked child,' she yelled, 'you've eaten those, too!'

'Oh no I didn't,' said Karlson indignantly. 'But you always have to blame me.'

At that moment they heard footsteps climbing the stairs. It must be Uncle Julius at last. Smidge was glad that this put an end to the quarrel, and glad that Uncle Julius wasn't lost in the bustle of the big city.

'Oh good,' said Smidge, 'he's found his way home after all!'

'Only because he had a trail to follow,' said Karlson, 'otherwise he'd never have made it!'

'What sort of trail?' asked Smidge.

'A trail that I made,' said Karlson, 'because I'm the nicest Karlson in the world!'

But then the front door bell rang. Miss Crawley went to open the door and Smidge followed her to say hello to Uncle Julius.

'Welcome home, Mr Janson,' said Miss Crawley.

'We thought perhaps you'd got lost,' said Smidge.

But Uncle Julius didn't answer either of them.

'Why,' he asked severely, 'are there drop scones hanging on every single door handle in this block of flats?'

He looked accusingly at Smidge, and Smidge muttered anxiously:

'Maybe the Sandman . . . '

Then he turned on his heels and dashed straight

back to the kitchen to give Karlson a piece of his mind.

There was no Karlson in the kitchen. There were only two empty plates and one lonely little blob of jam, left on the oilcloth at Karlson's place.

Uncle Julius and Smidge and Miss Crawley had black pudding for lunch. That's quite tasty, too.

It was Smidge who had to run down to the local shop to buy the black pudding in a hurry. He didn't protest when Miss Crawley sent him, because he was rather keen to see what all those door handles looked like with their drop scones.

But there were no drop scones there. He ran down the stairs and checked every single handle on every floor of the block, but as far as he could see there wasn't a single drop scone anywhere, and he began to think Uncle Julius had imagined it all.

Until he got down to the ground floor. On the very bottom step sat Karlson. He was eating drop scones.

'Drop scones are yummy,' he said. 'And he can manage without his trail now, Jules the Elf, because he'll know the way after today.'

Then he gave a sudden snort.

'It wasn't fair, what Creepy Crawley said! She accused me of eating up the drop scones, when I was as innocent as a lamb. So I might as well eat them up anyway!'

Smidge had to laugh.

'You're the world's best drop-scone eater, Karlson,' he said.

But then he remembered something and grew very serious. He remembered the awful thing Spike and Rollo had said. At last he could tell Karlson.

'I think they're going to try to catch you tonight,' said Smidge in alarm. 'Do you know what that means?'

Karlson licked his greasy fingers and gave a contented little purr.

'It means we'll have a very merry evening,' he said. 'Whoop, whoop! Whoop, whoop!'

KARLSON IS THE WORLD'S BEST SNORE EXPERT

Eventually it was evening. Karlson had kept out of the way all afternoon. He probably wanted Creepy Crawley to have a good, long rest after that drop scone tirritation.

Smidge had been to the railway museum with Uncle Julius. That was something they both liked. Then they had come home to dinner with Miss Crawley and it had all stayed very quiet—no Karlson anywhere. But when Smidge went to his room after dinner, there was Karlson.

To be honest, Smidge was not very pleased to see him.

'You take way too many risks,' he said. 'Why are you here?'

'Don't ask such daft questions,' said Karlson. 'Because I'm staying the night with you, of course!'

Smidge sighed. All day he'd been worrying without saying anything, and brooding about how to keep Karlson safe from Spike and Rollo. He had thought and thought—perhaps he should ring the police? No, because then he'd have to explain that Spike and Rollo wanted to kidnap Karlson, and he couldn't do that. Could he ask Uncle Julius for help? No, because he would ring the police *immediately*, and then Smidge would have to explain about Spike and Rollo wanting to kidnap Karlson anyway, which was no help.

Karlson certainly hadn't been brooding or thinking, and he wasn't at all anxious now, either. He was calmly taking a look to see how much the peach stone had grown. But Smidge was really anxious.

'I just don't know what we're going to do,' he said.

'To Spike and Rollo, you mean?' said Karlson. 'But I do know. I've told you there are three ways—tirritation, jiggery-pokery, and figuration, and I'm planning to use all three of them.'

Smidge thought the fourth way would be the best; that is, if Karlson stayed at home in his house on the roof, for just this one night, curled up under his covers as quiet as a little mouse. But Karlson said that of all the ridiculous ways he had heard of, that was the most ridiculous ever.

Smidge still wouldn't give up. Uncle Julius had given him a bag of toffees, and it occurred to him that he might be able to use them to bribe Karlson. He dangled the bag in front of Karlson's nose as invitingly as he could, and said slyly:

'I'll give you the whole bag if you fly home and go to bed!'

But Karlson brushed Smidge's hand aside.

'Goodness me, what a horrible boy you are,' he said. 'Keep your wretched toffees! Don't go imagining *I* want them!'

He pouted sullenly and went over and sat down

on a stool in the corner of the room, as far away as he could get.

'You can count me out if you're going to be so horrible,' he said. 'You can just count me out!'

Smidge was desperate. He simply hated it when Karlson said 'Count me out'. Smidge quickly said he was sorry, and tried everything he could to get Karlson back in a good mood, but nothing worked. Karlson went on sulking.

'Well, I've run out of ideas, now,' said Smidge in the end.

'But I've got one,' said Karlson. 'I'm not a hundred per cent sure, but I think I might decide you can count me in if you give me some little something . . . er . . . maybe I could have that bag of toffees, for instance!'

So Smidge gave him the bag of toffees and then Karlson counted himself in. And he planned on being counted in all night long.

'Whoop, whoop,' he said. 'You just wouldn't believe how much you can count me in!'

Since Karlson insisted on staying the night, there was nothing for it but to make up a bed on the sofa for himself again, thought Smidge, and was about to set to work. But then Karlson said there was no point! This wasn't going to be a night for sleeping— just the opposite.

'Though I am hoping Creepy Crawley and Jules the Elf are going to drop off before long, because we need to get started,' said Karlson.

And Uncle Julius did go to bed early. He must have been tired after all the disturbances of last night, and all the things he'd done today. Miss Crawley certainly needed her sleep, too, after all that exhausting bun and drop-scone tirritation. She soon retired to her room—well, it was Sally's room really. That was where Mum had decided Miss Crawley would sleep this time.

Before bed, they came in to say goodnight to Smidge, Uncle Julius and Miss Crawley, but Karlson stayed out of sight in the wardrobe. Even he could see it was the most sensible thing to do.

Uncle Julius yawned.

'I hope the Sandman will come soon and let us all go to sleep under his red umbrella,' he said.

You'll be lucky, thought Smidge, but all he said was:

'Goodnight, Uncle Julius, sleep well! Goodnight, Miss Crawley.'

'You get straight off to bed now,' Miss Crawley told him.

And then they were gone.

Smidge got out of his clothes and put on his pyjamas. It would be best that way, he thought, in case Miss Crawley or Uncle Julius came dashing along in the middle of the night and happened to see him.

Smidge and Karlson played beggar-my-neighbour while they were waiting for Uncle Julius and Miss Crawley to fall asleep. But Karlson was a terrible cheat, and he had to win all the time, otherwise Smidge could count him out, he said. Smidge did his best to let Karlson win all the time, but when it finally seemed he was going to lose one round after all, Karlson briskly raked all the cards into a heap and said:

'We haven't got time to play this any more. We've got to get on with things!'

By then, Uncle Julius and Miss Crawley were

asleep—without the help of the Sandman or his umbrella. Karlson kept himself amused for quite a while, running from one bedroom door to the other and comparing their snores.

'The world's best snore expert, guess who that is,' he said delightedly, and then he did imitations for Smidge of how Uncle Julius and Miss Crawley snored.

'Grrrr-few-few-few, that's how Jules the Elf goes. But Creepy Crawley snores like this: Grrr-ashh, Grrrr-ashh!'

Then Karlson remembered something. He still had lots of toffees left, despite having given Smidge one and gobbled ten himself, and now he needed to hide the bag somewhere, he said, to have his hands free to get on with things. But it had to be an absolutely secure place.

'Since there are burglars coming,' he said. 'Haven't you got a safe in this flat?'

Smidge said that if they had, he would have locked Karlson in it in the first place, but sadly they hadn't.

Karlson thought for a while.

'I'll put the bag in with Jules the Elf,' he said. 'Because when the burglars hear the grrr-few-few-few, they'll think it's a tiger and won't dare go in.'

He gently opened the door to the main bedroom. The sound of grrr-few-few-few grew louder. Karlson sniggered in delight and vanished through the door with the toffee bag. Smidge stood waiting outside.

After a while, Karlson emerged again. Without the bag. But clutching Uncle Julius's false teeth.

'Oh, Karlson, no,' said Smidge. 'Why have you taken those?'

'You don't think I'd leave my toffees in the care of anyone with teeth, do you?' asked Karlson. 'Say Jules the Elf wakes up in the night and spots the bag! If he's got his teeth handy, he'll start chewing and never stop. But now he can't, luckily.'

'Uncle Julius would never do that,' Smidge assured him. 'He'd never take a single toffee that wasn't his.'

'Don't be daft, he might think some messenger from fairyland had been there and left the bag for him,' said Karlson.

'I don't think so, since he bought it in the first place,' objected Smidge, but Karlson didn't want to listen.

'I need these teeth, see,' he said. He needed a stout piece of rope too, he said, so Smidge crept into the kitchen and got a length of washing line from the broom cupboard.

'What's it for?' asked Smidge.

'I'm going to make a burglar trap,' said Karlson. 'A terrible, fearsome, deadly burglar trap!'

And he showed Smidge where he was going to

131

make it, too—in the archway where the little lobby just inside the front door went through to the hall.

'Just there,' said Karlson.

In the hall, on either side of the archway, stood a pair of solid chairs, and Karlson rigged up a simple but clever burglar trap by stretching the washing line low—almost at floor level—across the archway and tying it firmly to the sturdy chair legs. Anyone coming from the lobby to the hall in the dark would be bound to trip over the line, for sure.

Smidge remembered Spike and Rollo coming to burgle the flat the year before. They had got in by poking a long wire through the letterbox, and then managing to pick the lock. That was probably what they were planning this time, too, and it would jolly well serve them right if they tripped over the washing line.

Smidge chuckled quietly to himself, and then had a thought that reassured him even more.

'I've been going around worrying for nothing,' he said, 'because Bumble will bark loud enough to wake the whole house, and then they'll run away, Spike and Rollo.'

Karlson stared at him as if he couldn't believe his ears.

'You mean to say,' he said severely, 'I've made this burglar trap for nothing? And do you suppose I'm going to stand for that, eh? No, that dog has got to go, and pronto!'

This made Smidge cross.

'What do you mean? And what exactly am I supposed to do with him, had you thought of that?'

Karlson said Bumble could sleep up at his house. He could lie on Karlson's kitchen settee and have a lovely long sleep, while Karlson was out jiggery-poking. And when Bumble got out of bed the next morning, he'd find himself up to his knees in best mince, promised Karlson, if only Smidge would see reason.

But Smidge didn't want to see that sort of reason. He thought it was treating Bumble shamefully, sending him away like that. And besides, it would be really useful to have a barking dog when Spike and Rollo turned up.

'Fine, you go ahead and spoil everything,' said Karlson bitterly. 'Don't ever let me have any fun, oh no, just stop me all the time so I can't do a single bit of tirritation or jiggery-pokery or figurating, go on! As long as your precious doggy gets to bark his head off all night.'

'But you know . . . ' began Smidge, but Karlson interrupted him.

'Count me out! You'll have to find your own jiggery-pokers from now on, because you can just count me out!'

Bumble growled disapprovingly when Smidge came and pulled him out of

his basket just when he'd dozed off, and the last Smidge saw of his dog as Karlson flew off into the air with him was a pair of big, surprised eyes.

'Don't be afraid, Bumble! I'll come and get you very soon,' cried Smidge as comfortingly as he could.

Karlson came back a couple of minutes later, all bright and cheery.

'Guess what Bumble said to tell you? It's so *nice* up

here at your house, Karlson, he said. Can't I be *your* dog instead?'

'Ha ha, I bet he didn't!'

Smidge was laughing because he knew very well whose dog Bumble was, and Bumble knew it too.

'Anyway, it's all going to be fine now,' said Karlson. 'I mean to say, you know that when there are two good friends like you and me, one of them has to fit in with the other one and do what the other one wants sometimes.'

'Yes, but you're always the other one,' said Smidge with a giggle, but he did wonder what Karlson thought he was doing. Surely absolutely anyone could see that on a night like this, the best thing would be for Karlson to be lying up there on his kitchen settee with the covers over his head, while Bumble stayed down here and scared off Spike and Rollo by barking loudly enough to shake the whole house? But now Karlson had managed to get it all completely the other way round, and had almost convinced Smidge that it was for the best. And Smidge was quite ready to believe him, because deep down he was keen for an adventure and couldn't wait to see what sort of jiggery-pokery Karlson would come up with this time.

Karlson wanted to get on with things, because he thought Spike and Rollo might come any time.

'I'm going to jiggery-poke something to frighten the life out of them from the word go,' he said. 'We don't need any silly little dog for that, believe me.'

He dashed off to the kitchen and started rooting about in the broom cupboard. Smidge anxiously asked him to keep the noise down, because Miss Crawley was asleep in Sally's room right next door. Karlson hadn't thought of that.

'Go and listen at the doors,' he commanded Smidge. 'If the grrrr-few-few-few or the grr-ashh, grrrr-ashh stop, you must tell me, because that means trouble's brewing.'

He thought for a moment.

'I'll tell you what you'll have to do if that happens,' he said. 'You'll have to start snoring as hard as you can. Like this: grrr-aaah, grrr-aaah!'

'How will that help?' asked Smidge.

'Well, if it's Jules the Elf who's woken up, he'll

think he can hear Creepy Crawley. But I'll know the grrr-aaah is you, and realize someone's awake and there's trouble brewing, so then I'll sneak into the broom cupboard and hide, hee hee; the world's best jiggery-poker, guess who that is!'

'But if Spike and Rollo do come, what shall I do then?' asked Smidge, rather alarmed, because it wouldn't be much fun on his own in the hall when the burglars came, with Karlson tucked away in the kitchen.

'You'll have to start snoring then, too,' said Karlson. 'Like this: grr-her-her-her, grr-her-her-her.'

It was just as hard as learning your times tables, thought Smidge, to memorize all this grrrr-few-few-few and grr-ashh, and grrr-aaah and grr-her-her-her, but he promised to do his best.

Karlson went over to the towel rack and grabbed all the tea towels.

'There aren't enough towels here,' he said. 'But I bet there are some more in the bathroom.'

'What are you going to do?' asked Smidge.

'Make a mummy,' said Karlson. 'A terrible, fearsome, deadly mummy!'

Smidge didn't really know what mummies were, but he had an idea they were something you found in ancient royal graves in Egypt. He was pretty sure they were dead kings and queens wrapped up in a stiff sort of parcel, with staring eyes. Dad had told him about them once. The kings and queens had been embalmed, which meant they could be kept exactly as they were when they were alive, and then they were wrapped in layer after layer of strips of cloth, Dad had said. But Karlson wasn't an embalmer, thought Smidge, and he asked in astonishment.

'*How* are you going to make a mummy?'

'I shall wrap up the carpet beater, but don't you worry about that. You go and stand on guard and do your bit, and I'll get on with mine.'

Smidge stood on guard. He listened at both doors and heard some very reassuring snores: grr-few-few-few and grr-ashh exactly as it should be. But then Uncle Julius must have started having a nightmare, because his snores suddenly went strange and moany, grrr-mmmm, grrr-mmmm, not at all like the calm murmur of few-few-few. Smidge wondered if he ought to go and tell the world's best snore expert in the kitchen, but just as he was thinking about it, he heard urgent, running footsteps and then a dreadful crash and then a string of curses. They came from the burglar trap. Oh help, it must be Spike and Rollo! At that moment Smidge realized to his horror that grrr-ashh had stopped. Oh help, whatever should he do? He desperately went over all the orders Karlson had given him, and then made a feeble little grr-aaah, quickly followed by an equally feeble grr-her-her-her, but neither of them sounded like snores at all.

He tried again.

'Grrr . . . '

'Shut up,' hissed somebody over by the burglar trap, and through the gloom he noticed something small and fat crawling on the floor between the two upturned chairs, and trying to struggle to its feet. It was Karlson.

Smidge ran over and picked up the chairs so Karlson could get up. But Karlson wasn't in the least grateful. He was hopping mad.

'It's your fault,' he hissed. 'Didn't I tell you to fetch me some towels from the bathroom?'

Karlson hadn't told him that at all. Poor Karlson, he had forgotten that to get to the bathroom you had to go through the burglar trap, but Smidge really couldn't help that.

There was no time to argue about whose fault it was, anyway, because just then they heard the rattle of Miss Crawley's bedroom door handle. There wasn't a moment to lose.

Karlson sped off to the kitchen and Smidge ran like mad into his room and threw himself into bed.

Not a second too soon. He pulled the covers up to his chin and tried to do a believable little grr-aaah, but it didn't sound right at all, so he stopped and just lay there listening to Miss Crawley, who came into his room and over to the bed. He squinted cautiously through his eyelashes and saw her standing there in her nightgown, white in the semi-darkness of the summer night. Yes, she was just standing there, looking down at him with concern, and he felt his whole body begin to itch.

'Don't try pretending you're asleep,' said Miss Crawley, but she didn't sound cross. 'Did that clap of thunder wake you, too?' she asked, and Smidge stammered:

'I . . . I think so.'

Miss Crawley nodded and seemed satisfied.

'I've felt all day that we were going to have a storm. There's been a strange, close feeling in the air. But you mustn't be afraid,' she said, and patted Smidge on the head. 'The thunder rumbles but the lightning never strikes here, in the city.'

Then off she went. Smidge lay in bed for a long while, not daring to move. But, eventually, he crept out of bed. He wondered uneasily what had happened to Karlson, and made his way to the kitchen as quietly as he could.

The first thing he saw was the mummy. Ye gods and little fishes, as Uncle Julius would say, he saw the mummy! It was sitting on the draining board, and beside it stood Karlson, proud as punch, spotlighting it with the torch he had found in the broom cupboard.

'Isn't she smart?' he said.

She—so it must be a queen mummy, thought Smidge. But she was certainly a rather round and

chubby queen, because Karlson had wrapped the carpet beater in every last towel and tea towel he could
lay his hands on. He had made a face for the 'head' of
the carpet beater by stretching a towel over it, and
drawing two big, staring black eyes on it. But the
mummy had teeth, too. Real teeth. Uncle Julius's
teeth. They were pressed into the towel and some-
how held in place by the curved cane shape of the
carpet beater, but to fix them even more securely,
Karlson had put a sticking plaster at each corner of

the mummy's mouth. It really was a terrible, fear-some, deadly mummy, but it still made Smidge giggle.

'Why's she got those plasters?' he asked.

'I expect she cut herself shaving,' said Karlson, patting the mummy on the cheek. 'Whoop, whoop, she looks so much like my mum that I'm thinking of calling her Ma.'

He took the mummy in his arms and carried her out to the hall.

'It will be fun for Spike and Rollo to meet Ma,' he said.

Karlson Jiggery-pokes Best in the Dark

A long piece of wire came creeping through the letterbox.

You couldn't see it, because it was pitch dark in the little lobby, but you could hear the rattle and the scrape. Yes, it was them, Spike and Rollo!

Smidge and Karlson were sitting waiting, squeezed under the little, round table in the hall. They had been sitting there for at least an hour. Smidge had even dozed off for a while. But he came to with a jerk when the letterbox rattled: here they were! Smidge was suddenly wide awake, and so scared he felt a shiver run down his spine, but in the darkness he heard Karlson give a happy purr.

'Whoop, whoop,' he whispered, 'here we go!'

Fancy it being so easy to unlock a door with just a piece of wire! Now the door was slowly opening, someone was coming in, someone was in the lobby—Smidge held his breath, this was really awful! They heard whispers and stealthy foot-steps . . . But then a crash, oh what a crash, and two muffled cries! And then a sudden, short flash of Karlson's torch from under the table, so the light had shone for a moment on a terrible, deadly mummy, propped against the wall and grinning its fearsome grin with Uncle Julius's teeth. The light was abruptly switched off again. There were more shrieks from the burglar trap, a bit louder this time.

Then everything happened at once. Smidge couldn't keep up with it all. He heard doors open, as Uncle Julius and Miss Crawley came to investigate, and at the same time he heard swift feet running back into the lobby, and Ma shuffling across the floor as Karlson reeled her in with Bumble's lead, which he had tied round her neck. He also heard

Miss Crawley keep flicking the switch to put the light on, but Karlson had unscrewed all the fuses in the electric meter in the kitchen—you jiggery-poke best in the dark, he had said—so that left Miss Crawley and Uncle Julius helpless, without any light.

'What a dreadful storm,' said Miss Crawley. 'What a crack of thunder, eh? No wonder the power's gone off.'

'Was that really thunder?' said Uncle Julius. 'I thought it sounded like something quite different.'

But Miss Crawley assured him she recognized thunder when she heard it.

'What else could it have been?' she asked.

'I thought perhaps it was some mystical beings from fairyland, holding a meeting here tonight,' said Uncle Julius.

What he actually said, lisping so much that his spit sprayed everywhere, was 'thome mythical beingth'. This was because he hadn't got his teeth in, Smidge realized, but he immediately forgot about it again. He hadn't time to think about anything except Spike and Rollo, now: where had they

147

got to? Had they gone for good? He hadn't heard the front door close behind them, so presumably they were still lurking in the dark in the lobby, hidden behind the coats perhaps—how awful!

'Easy now, take it easy,' whispered Karlson. 'They'll be back any minute.'

'Well, I don't know, it'th jutht one thing after another,' said Uncle Julius. 'No chanth of a dethent night'th thleep in thith plathe.'

Then he and Miss Crawley both went back to their rooms, and it all went quiet. Karlson and Smidge stayed under the table, waiting. They waited for ever, it seemed to Smidge. Grr-few-few-few and grr-ashh started up again, gently and in the distance, of course, but still a sign that Uncle Julius and Miss Crawley had settled down.

And then, sure enough, Spike and Rollo came padding out of the darkness again. They came very cautiously, and at the burglar trap they stopped and listened. You could hear their breathing in the darkness. It was awful. Then they switched on their torches; oh yes, they had torches, too. Smidge closed his eyes, as if he thought that would make him more invisible. The tablecloth hung right down to the floor, luckily, but how easily Spike and Rollo would be able to find them under there, Smidge and Karlson and Ma. Smidge squeezed his eyes tight shut and held his breath. And he heard Spike and Rollo whispering to each other, right beside him.

'Did you see the ghost, too?' asked Spike.

'You bet I did,' said Rollo. 'It was over by that wall, but now it's gone.'

'Well, this is the most haunted flat in the whole of Stockholm, we know that from last time,' said Spike.

'Oh blow it, let's get out of here,' said Rollo.

But Spike didn't want to.

'Not on your life! For ten thousand kronor I can put up with dozens of ghosts, sure as my name's Spike!'

He quietly picked up the chairs from the burglar trap and put them aside. That was so they wouldn't be in the way if he happened to need to leave in a hurry, and he wondered crossly what sort of horrid little children lived here, since their idea of fun was to trip up visitors.

'I went flat on my face and bashed my eye,' he said. 'I shall have a lovely bruise, thanks to those mangy brats!'

Then he shone his torch into every nook and cranny again.

'Let's find out where all these doors lead and then we'll start the search,' he said.

The beam of light played to and fro, and every time it came near the table, Smidge shut his eyes and made himself as small as he could. He frantically pulled in his feet, which felt so gigantic he was sure there wasn't room for them under the table, and they would stick out so far that Spike and Rollo would see them.

While all this was going on, Smidge noticed Karlson picking up Ma again. The beam of torchlight had moved on now, and it was dark under the table, but just light enough for Smidge to see Karlson shoving Ma out from under the cloth and propping her up with her back to the table. There she stood as the torchlight came sweeping past again and caught her right in the middle of her fearsome grin. And then once more they heard two muffled cries and the sound of feet dashing back to the lobby.

Karlson leapt into action.

'Come on,' he panted in Smidge's ear, and then crawled as fast as a hedgehog across the hall with Ma dragging behind him, and zipped out of sight into Smidge's room. Smidge crawled after him.

'What a dim pair,' said Karlson, closing the door behind them. 'Not being able to tell the difference between ghosts and mummies, I call that really dim.'

He cautiously opened the door a crack and listened for sounds from the hall. Smidge listened too, longing to hear the front door close behind Spike and Rollo, but that was too much to hope for. They were still out there, worse luck, and he could hear them talking to each other in low voices.

'Ten thousand kronor,' said Spike, 'don't forget! I shan't let any ghost scare me, I can tell you.'

A little time passed. Karlson kept listening intently.

'They're in with Jules the Elf,' he said. 'Whoop whoop, now we can really get to work!'

He took Ma off her lead and laid her tenderly in Smidge's bed.

'Heysan hopsan, Ma. You can get a bit of sleep at last,' he said, and tucked her in like a mother tucking in her child for the night. Then he beckoned Smidge over.

'Look, isn't she sweet?' he said, and shone the torch on his mummy.

Smidge gave a shudder. Lying there staring up at the ceiling with her staring black eyes and fearsome grin, Ma would have scared the life out of anybody. But Karlson gave her a contented pat and then pulled the sheet and blanket up over her face. He also took the bedspread that Miss Crawley had folded up and left on a chair when she came to say goodnight to Smidge, and spread it carefully over the bed, probably so Ma wouldn't get cold, thought Smidge with a giggle. Now all that was to be seen of her was a plump, rounded shape making a mound in the bedclothes.

'Heysan hopsan, Smidge,' said Karlson. 'It's time for you to get a bit of sleep, too, I think.'

'But where?' asked Smidge uneasily, because he most definitely didn't want to sleep beside Ma. 'I can't get into my bed when Ma's . . . '

'No, but *under* it you can.' And he crawled under the bed as fast as a hedgehog, and Smidge went in after him, as quickly as he could.

'Now I'll show you what a typical spy's snore is like,' said Karlson.

'Do spies snore in a special way, then?' asked Smidge in surprise.

'Yes, they do such a crafty, sinister snore that it could drive you mad. Like this: uuuuurh, uuuuurh, uuuuurh!'

The spy snores droned menacingly, rising and

falling and growling. It really did sound crafty and sinister. And also quite loud. This made Smidge anxious.

'Be quiet! Spike and Rollo might come!'

'Exactly, and that's why we need some spy snores,' said Karlson.

At that very moment Smidge heard someone turn the door handle. The door opened a little way. A beam of light shone through the gap, and Spike and Rollo tiptoed in after it.

Karlson snored his crafty, sinister snore, and Smidge squeezed his eyes tight shut. Not that he really needed to, because the bedspread was hanging down to the floor and protecting him and Karlson from any inquisitive beams of light or prying eyes. And that was the way Karlson had planned it, of course.

'Uuuuurh,' snored Karlson.

'We've come to the right place at last,' said Spike under his breath. 'No kid snores like that, so it must be him. Look at that fat lump lying there, yeah, it must be him.'

There was an angry 'Uuuuurh', from Karlson. He didn't want to be called a fat lump. You could hear that from the snore.

'Have you got the handcuffs ready?' asked Rollo. 'We'd better clap them on before he wakes up.'

They heard the rustle of the bedspread, and then a gasp from Spike and Rollo. They must have seen the fearsome, deadly mummy with her head resting on the pillow, thought Smidge. But they were obviously used to her now, and not quite so easily scared, because they didn't cry out or run away, but just gave a sort of gasp.

'Huh, it's just a doll,' said Spike, a bit embarrassed . . . 'and, blimey, what a doll,' he said, and must have covered her up again, because the bedspread rustled back into place.

'Er . . . Spike,' said Rollo, 'how do you reckon the doll got here, though? She was out in the hall just now, wasn't she?'

'You're right,' said Spike thoughtfully. 'And who's that snoring, come to think of it?'

There was no time for Spike to find out, because there came the sound of footsteps from the hall. Smidge recognized Miss Crawley's heavy tread, and thought nervously that they were in for a worse din than any clap of thunder.

But they weren't.

'Quick, into the drawerwobe,' hissed Spike, and before Smidge could blink, Spike and Rollo disappeared into the wardrobe.

Karlson leapt into action. As quick as a hedgehog he crawled over to the wardrobe and locked Spike and Rollo in. Then he crept back to his hiding place under the bed, and the next second Miss Crawley stepped into the room, looking almost as if she was dressed up for a Lucia procession, in her white gown and with a lighted candle in her hand.

Smidge could tell she was right by the bed, because her big toe was sticking under the bedspread, and he heard her stern voice high above his head.

'Smidge, was that you in my room just now, waving a torch about?'

'N-no, it wasn't me,' stammered Smidge without thinking.

'Why aren't you asleep then?' asked Miss Crawley suspiciously, and added:

'Don't talk from under the covers, I can't hear what you're saying!'

There was a rustle as she pulled back the bedspread

from what she thought was Smidge's face. And then they heard an almighty howl. Poor Miss Crawley, she wasn't as used to seeing fearsome, deadly mummies as Spike and Rollo, thought Smidge. He knew it was time to come out and show himself. She would find him anyway, and he needed her help with Spike and Rollo. He'd got to get them out of the wardrobe, even if it meant all the secrets in the world being given away in the process.

So Smidge crawled out.

'Don't be scared,' he said anxiously. 'Ma isn't dangerous, but I'm afraid there are two burglars in the wardrobe.'

Miss Crawley was still in a state of shock from seeing Ma. She had her hand pressed to her heart and was breathing heavily, but when Smidge mentioned burglars in the wardrobe, it seemed to make her cross.

'What nonsense is this you're making up? Burglars in the wardrobe, don't talk rubbish!'

But to be on the safe side, she went over to the wardrobe door and asked:

'Is there anybody there?'

There was no answer, and that made her even crosser.

'Answer me! Is there anyone there? If you're not there, you could at least say so!'

Then she heard scuffling sounds from inside the wardrobe, and realized Smidge had been telling the truth.

'Oh, you brave boy,' she exclaimed. 'A little scrap like you managing to lock in two big, tough burglars, oh, how brave!'

Then there was some thumping under the bed, and Karlson came crawling out.

'Oh no he didn't,' said Karlson. 'It was me, so there!'

He glared angrily from Miss Crawley to Smidge and back again.

'And I'm brave and great in every way, just remember that,' he said. 'And thoroughly clever and rather handsome too, by the way, and certainly not a fat lump, so there!'

Miss Crawley was furious when she saw Karlson.

'You . . . you . . . ' she cried, but then she recalled that this wasn't the time or place to be telling

Karlson off about the drop scone episode. There were more important things to think about. She turned urgently to Smidge.

'Run in and wake Uncle Julius, so we can ring the police . . . oh, I'd better just put my dressing gown on first,' she said with a horrified glance at her nightdress. And she dashed off. Smidge darted off too, but first he grabbed the teeth from Ma. He knew that just now, Uncle Julius needed them more.

In the main bedroom, grrr-few-few-few was in full swing. Uncle Julius was sleeping as soundly as a baby.

It was just beginning to get light. In the grey gleam, Smidge could see the glass of water standing in its usual place on the bedside table. He popped the teeth into it, and they made a little splash. Next to the glass were Uncle Julius's spectacles and Karlson's bag of toffees. Smidge took the bag and put it in his pyjama pocket to give to Karlson. There was no need for Uncle Julius to see it when he woke up, and start wondering how it had got there.

Smidge had a feeling there was usually something

else on the bedside table—oh yes, Uncle Julius's watch and wallet. They weren't there now. But Smidge couldn't worry about them now. His job was to wake Uncle Julius, and so he did.

Uncle Julius woke up with a start.

'What ith it now?'

He quickly fished out his teeth and put them in his mouth, and then said:

'I can't wait to get straight home to Västergötland after all the disturbed nights in this place . . . and then I shall sleep for sixteen hours at a stretch, so there!'

That was a sentence he really did need his teeth for, thought Smidge, and he started explaining to Uncle Julius why he'd got to come, right this minute.

Uncle Julius strode off as fast as he could, with Smidge running after him, and Miss Crawley came loping from the other direction, and they all stormed into Smidge's room at the same time.

'Oh, Mr Janson, burglars, just think!' cried Miss Crawley.

The first thing Smidge noticed was that there was no sign of Karlson in the room. The window was open. He must have flown home, thank goodness for that! So now Spike and Rollo wouldn't have to see him after all, and nor would the police. It was almost too good to be true!

'They're in the wardrobe,' said Miss Crawley, sounding scared but pleased at the same time. But Uncle Julius pointed to the fat lump in Smidge's bed and said:

'Wouldn't it be as well to wake Smidge up first?'

Then he looked in astonishment at Smidge, standing beside him.

'Though I see he's already awake—but who's that in his bed, then?'

Miss Crawley shuddered. She knew very well what was in the bed. There were even more gruesome things than burglars here.

'Something ghastly,' she said. 'It's something altogether ghastly! From fairyland, I dare say!'

Uncle Julius's eyes began to gleam. He wasn't frightened, oh no. He patted the lump that was sticking up under the bedclothes.

'Something fat and ghastly from fairyland, this I *must* see, before I deal with any burglars!'

He briskly pulled back the bedspread.

'Hee hee,' said Karlson and sat up in bed, beaming, 'it wasn't anybody from fairyland, so there, because it's just little me, hah! What a let-down, eh?'

Miss Crawley gave Karlson a furious glare, and Uncle Julius seemed most disappointed.

'So you have that boy here overnight, too?' he asked.

'It seems so, but I shall be wringing his neck as soon as I get a minute,' declared Miss Crawley. But then she gripped Uncle Julius's arm anxiously.

'Oh, Mr Janson, we'd better ring the police!'

Then something unexpected happened. They heard a gruff voice from the wardrobe, and it said:

'Open up in the name of the law! It's the police!'

This amazed Miss Crawley, Uncle Julius, and Smidge, but made Karlson very annoyed.

'The police . . . Try pulling the other one, you stupid thuggy thieves!'

But then Spike shouted from the wardrobe that there were very stiff penalties for locking up police officers who came to arrest dangerous spies—yes, they were being very cunning, thought Smidge.

'Now please just open up,' cried Spike.

So Uncle Julius obediently went and unlocked the wardrobe. Out stepped Spike and Rollo, and they seemed so angry and policelike that Uncle Julius and Miss Crawley were genuinely alarmed.

'But you police officers,' said Uncle Julius hesitantly, 'shouldn't you have uniforms?'

'No, because we're from the secret service,' said Rollo.

'And we've come to arrest him,' said Spike, pointing to Karlson. 'He's a very dangerous spy!'

Hearing that, Miss Crawley gave one of her dreadful cackles.

'Spy! Him? Not likely! He's one of Smidge's horrible schoolfriends!'

Karlson leapt out of bed.

'And I'm the best in the class, what's more,' he said eagerly, 'oh yes I am, because I can waggle my ears and . . . er . . . do addition too, of course!'

But Spike didn't believe him. Brandishing the handcuffs, he moved threateningly towards Karlson. Closer and closer he came, but then Karlson gave him a sound kick on the shin. Spike let out a string of swearwords and hopped around on one leg.

'You'll have a nice bruise there, all right,' said Karlson smugly, and Smidge thought bruises must be something burglars got plenty of. Spike's eye had almost swollen shut now, and had turned a bluey-black colour. It served him right, thought Smidge, for coming in here and trying to kidnap Smidge's own Karlson and sell him for ten thousand kronor. Beastly burglars, Smidge hoped they'd soon be a huge mass of bruises!

'They're not policemen, they're lying,' he said. 'I know they're thieves and burglars.'

Uncle Julius scratched the back of his neck, rather perplexed.

'We need to get to the bottom of this,' he said.

He suggested they should all assemble in the sitting room, and sort out whether Spike and Rollo were burglars or not.

It was almost morning and getting much lighter. The stars had faded from the sky outside the sitting room window, a new day was dawning, and Smidge was longing for nothing more than the chance to go to bed at last, instead of sitting here listening to Spike's and Rollo's lies.

'Didn't you read in the paper about the spy flying around the Vasa district?' said Rollo, taking a newspaper cutting out of his pocket.

But this made Uncle Julius look very superior.

'You shouldn't believe all the rubbish they write in the papers,' he said. 'But by all means let me have another look at that. Hang on, I must just go and get my spectacles!'

He went off to his bedroom, but he was back almost immediately, and he was very angry.

'Fine policemen you are,' he roared. 'You've stolen my wallet and watch. Now just you give them back, right now!'

But then it was Spike's and Rollo's turn to be very indignant. It was extremely dangerous to accuse police officers of stealing wallets and watches, maintained Rollo.

'It's called defamation, didn't you know?' said Spike. 'And you can end up in prison if you defame a police officer, didn't you know?'

Karlson seemed to have had a thought, because

he was suddenly in a great hurry. He rushed out just as Uncle Julius had done, and he was back just as fast, too, and spitting mad.

'And my bag of toffees,' he yelled, 'who took that?'

Spike advanced on him threateningly.

'Are you accusing us, eh?'

'Oh no, I'm not that stupid,' said Karlson. 'I shall be careful not to deflame anybody. But I can tell you this: if the person who took my bag doesn't give it straight back, he'll get a black eye the other side as well.'

Smidge quickly fished out the bag and handed it over to Karlson. 'I was looking after it for you.'

That made Spike sneer.

'There, see! But you're perfectly happy to accuse us of everything!'

Miss Crawley had been sitting there not saying anything, but now she wanted to play her part in the investigation.

'The watch and the wallet, I know who pinched them. He does nothing but steal stuff, buns and drop scones and anything he can find!'

She pointed at Karlson, and Karlson was livid.

'Now watch it! That's deflamation, and that's dangerous, didn't you know, silly woman!'

But Miss Crawley didn't care about Karlson. She wanted to have a serious talk to Uncle Julius now. It could well be true, she thought, that these gentlemen were from the secret police, because they looked pretty decent—well-dressed and everything. Thieves usually had ragged, patched clothes, Miss Crawley thought, having never seen a burglar for herself.

And that of course made Spike and Rollo very pleased with themselves. Spike said he had realized from the start what a wise and wonderful person this lady was, and he was delighted to have had a chance to meet her, he said. He even turned to Uncle Julius to back him up.

'I'm right, aren't I, she's charming.'

Uncle Julius didn't ever seem to have thought about it before, but now he was forced to agree, and that made Miss Crawley lower her eyes and blush bright red.

'Her, she's about as charming as a rattlesnake,'

muttered Karlson. He was sitting next to Smidge in a corner, noisily chomping his toffees, but when the bag was empty, he jumped up and began frisking round the room. It looked like some kind of game, but as he frisked he worked his way gradually towards Spike and Rollo, until he was standing right behind their chairs.

'A darling like that would be worth meeting again,' said Spike, and that made Miss Crawley go even redder and lower her eyes again.

'Yes yes, these charmings and darlings are all very well,' said Uncle Julius impatiently, 'but I want to know what's happened to my watch and wallet!'

Spike and Rollo didn't seem to hear. Anyway, Spike was so busy being charmed by Miss Crawley that he didn't care about anything else.

'Nice-looking, too, don't you think, Rollo?' he said, just quietly enough for Miss Crawley still to hear. 'Lovely eyes . . . And such a charmingly homely nose, the sort you can rely on in all weathers, don't you think, Rollo?'

Miss Crawley gave a start and her eyes almost popped out of her head.

'What on earth?' she cried. 'What did you say?'

Spike faltered.

'All I said was . . . ' he began, but Miss Crawley didn't let him get any further.

'So you're Mike, I suppose,' she said, and gave a smile almost as fearsome as Ma's, Smidge thought.

Spike was astonished.

'How do you know that? Have you heard of me?' Miss Crawley nodded grimly.

'Have I? Lordy lordy, I should say I have! And this must be Roland,' she said, pointing to Rollo.

'Yes, but how do you know? Have we got a mutual friend or something?' asked Spike, looking very pleased and expectant.

Miss Crawley nodded again, just as grimly.

'We certainly have! Miss Frida Crawley of Frey Street, that name rings a bell, doesn't it? She's someone with a nose to rely on in all weathers, if you recall, just like me.'

'Though yours isn't a homely potato but more of a cucumber with knobbly bits,' put in Karlson.

But Spike couldn't have been very interested in noses, because he didn't look happy any more.

Instead, he looked as though what he'd like most of all was to run away, and Rollo looked the same. But Karlson was standing right behind them. And suddenly a shot rang out, making Spike and Rollo jump out of their skins with fright.

'Don't shoot,' yelled Spike, because he could feel Karlson's index finger poking him in the back and thought it was a pistol.

'Cough up the wallet and the watch, then,' cried Karlson, 'or there'll be another bang.'

Spike and Rollo felt nervously in their jacket pockets, and what do you know, the wallet and the watch came flying through the air and landed in Uncle Julius's lap.

'There you are, fatso,' shouted Spike, and then both he and Rollo raced for the door like two streaks of lightning, before anyone could stop them.

But Miss Crawley dashed after them. She chased them right through the hall and through the lobby and out onto the landing, and shouted after them as they charged down the stairs:

'Frida's going to hear all about this, and lordy lordy, how glad she'll be!'

She took a couple of angry leaps forward, as if she was thinking of following them down the stairs, and shouted a final:

'Don't set foot in Frey Street again, because if you do, blood will be shed . . . Mark my words . . . blo-o-o-od!'

KARLSON REVEALS FAIRYLAND TO UNCLE JULIUS

After that night with Spike and Rollo, Karlson was even more bumptious than usual.

'Here comes the world's best Karlson,' was the cry Smidge woke to every morning, as Karlson came flying in. First thing every morning he dug up the peach stone to see how much it had grown, and then he paid his regular visit to the old mirror hanging above Smidge's chest of drawers. It wasn't a very big mirror, but Karlson flew to and fro in front of it so he could see as much of himself as possible. He couldn't fit his whole reflection into it in one go.

He hummed and sang as he flew, and you could
hear that what he was singing was a little, home-
made ditty in praise of himself.

'The world's best Karlson . . . humpty-tumpty-
hum . . . worth ten thousand kronor . . . scares off
burglars with his bistol . . . what a u-u-useless mirror
this is . . . you can't see much at all . . . of the world's
best Karlson in it . . . but the bit you can see is handsome . . . humpty-tumpty-hum . . . and perfectly
plump, oh yes . . . and great in every way.'

Smidge agreed. He thought Karlson was great in

every way. And the funny thing was, that even Uncle Julius was now quite taken with him. After all, it was actually Karlson who had rescued his wallet and watch. Uncle Julius didn't forget that sort of thing in a hurry. Miss Crawley, on the other hand, still had it in for Karlson, but Karlson didn't give a hoot, as long as he got fed at all the right times, which he did.

'If I don't get fed, you can count me out,' he had said, making it very plain.

Miss Crawley wished more than anything else in the world that she *could* count Karlson out, but there was no point when he had Smidge and Uncle Julius on his side. Miss Crawley growled every time he came dashing in and sat down at the table just as they were starting a meal, but there was nothing she could do. Karlson was there, and that was that.

He had slipped into the habit as something quite natural after the night with Spike and Rollo. He presumably thought even the crossest Creepy Crawley couldn't deny anything to a hero like him.

Karlson must have been tired after all his snore studies and sneaking and creeping and shooting that night, because it wasn't until almost dinnertime the next day that he came flying into Smidge's room and sniffed the air to see if he could detect any promising cooking smells from the kitchen.

Smidge, too, had had a good, long sleep, snoozing off again several times—with Bumble beside him in bed. It made you really sleepy, all this tussling with burglars at night, and he had only just woken up when Karlson came. He had been woken by an unusual and alarming sound from the kitchen. Miss Crawley was *singing* in there at the top of her voice. Smidge had never heard her do that before, and he really wished she would stop, because it was not a nice sound. For some reason she was in a particularly good mood that day. She had popped home to Frey Street to see Frida for a while in the morning, so maybe that was what had made her so perky, because her voice really boomed as she sang:

'Oh, Frida, that would be the best thing for you . . . ' she boomed, but before anyone could hear what was the best thing for Frida, Karlson dashed into the kitchen and cried:

'Stop! Stop! People might think I'm beating you if you go on howling like that.'

Miss Crawley stopped singing and truculently brought the beef stew to the table, and Uncle Julius came in and they all sat down to eat, and talked about the horrible events of the night and had rather a nice time together, Smidge thought. And Karlson liked the food and complimented Miss Crawley.

'Sometimes you actually manage to make a really delicious stew, quite by accident,' he said encouragingly.

Miss Crawley didn't answer him. She just swallowed a couple of times and pursed her lips.

The little chocolate puddings she had made for dessert were also very popular with Karlson. He gobbled one up before Smidge had time to take his first mouthful, and then announced:

'Well, a pudding like this is pretty yummy, but I know something twice as yummy!'

'What?' asked Smidge.

'Two puddings like this,' said Karlson, and grabbed another one. That meant Miss Crawley was left without one, because she had only made four. Karlson noticed her looking put out, and held up a warning finger.

'Remember there are some fatsoes at this table who could do with losing weight. Two, to be exact. I won't name any names but it's not me and it's not skinny here, either,' he said, indicating Smidge.

Miss Crawley pursed her lips even harder and still said not a word. Smidge cast an anxious glance at Uncle Julius, but he seemed not to have heard. He was too busy going on about how lazy the police in this city were. He had rung to report the burglary, but he might as well not have bothered. They had 315 other robberies to clear up first, they said, and incidentally, how much had been stolen, they wanted to know.

'But then I explained,' said Uncle Julius, 'that thanks to a certain brave and inventive little lad, those burglars had to go home to bed empty-handed.'

He looked approvingly at Karlson. Karlson preened himself like a cockerel, and gave Miss Crawley a triumphant nudge.

'What do you say to that, eh? The world's best Karlson, scares off burglars with his bistol,' he said.

Well, Uncle Julius had been scared senseless by

that pistol, too. Of course he was pleased and grateful to have his watch and wallet back, but he still didn't think little boys should go round with guns, and once Spike and Rollo had disappeared down the stairs at top speed, Smidge had had to do a lot of explaining before Uncle Julius would believe it was only a toy pistol Karlson had scared them off with.

After dinner, Uncle Julius went into the sitting room for a cigar. Miss Crawley did the washing up, and apparently not even Karlson could spoil her good mood for long, because she sang some more of her 'Oh Frida, that would be the best thing for you . . . ' But then she suddenly found there were no tea towels to dry up with, and that made her cross all over again.

'Can anybody work out where all the tea towels have gone?' she demanded, looking accusingly around the kitchen.

'Yes, *somebody* can, and that's the world's best towel finder,' said Karlson. 'How would it be if you *always* asked him when there's anything you don't know, you blockhead?'

Karlson headed off to Smidge's room and came

back carrying so many towels that they completely hid him from view. But what dirty, dusty towels they were, and that made Miss Crawley even more irate.

'*However* did the towels get like this?' she yelled.

'They've been on loan to fairyland,' said Karlson, 'and you know what, they never dust under their beds over there!'

The days went by. A postcard arrived from Mum and Dad. They were having a wonderful time on their cruise, and they hoped Smidge was enjoying himself, too, and Uncle Julius was keeping well and getting on all right at home with Smidge and Miss Crawley.

They didn't mention Karlson on the Roof, and that annoyed Karlson a lot.

'I'd send them a postcard, if I only had five öre for a stamp,' he said. 'And I'd write: That's right, don't you worry about whether Karlson is keeping well and is happy with Creepy Crawley, don't trouble yourselves, even though he's the one doing everything and scaring off burglars with his bistol and finding all the towels that get lost and checking up on Creepy Crawley for you and everything.'

Smidge was glad Karlson hadn't got five öre for a stamp, because he didn't think it would be a good idea for Mum and Dad to get a postcard like that. Smidge had emptied his piggy bank and given Karlson all the money in it, but Karlson had already spent the lot, and now he was cross.

'This is stupid,' he said. 'Here I am, worth ten thousand kronor, and yet I haven't got so much as five öre for a stamp. You don't think Uncle Julius might fancy buying my big toes, do you?'

Smidge didn't think so.

'But he does rather like me, you know,' said Karlson hopefully. Smidge still didn't think so, and then Karlson was offended and flew away home and didn't come back until the next meal was ready and Smidge pulled the bell cord and signalled to Karlson that it was time to come.

Mum and Dad were no doubt worried that Uncle Julius wouldn't like having Miss Crawley in the house, since they had written those things, thought Smidge, but they were wrong. In fact, Uncle Julius seemed to be getting on with Miss Crawley very well indeed. And as the days went by, Smidge noticed that they found more and more to talk about. They would often sit together in the sitting room, and you could hear Uncle Julius going on about fairyland and all manner of things, and Miss Crawley would answer him in such a polite, well-mannered way that you hardly believed she was the same person.

In the end, Karlson got suspicious. It was when Miss Crawley suddenly decided to close the door between the sitting room and the hall. It had always been there, you see, but none of the Stevensons ever pulled it shut. Maybe because the door had a little bolt on the inside, and once, when he was little, Smidge had bolted himself in, and then hadn't been able to get out. After that experience, Mum decided they could make do very well with a curtain. But now that Miss Crawley and Uncle Julius had coffee together in the sitting room in the evening, Miss Crawley suddenly wanted the door closed, and so did Uncle Julius, it turned out, because when Karlson came traipsing in, Uncle Julius said the boys would have to go and play somewhere else, as he now wanted to have his coffee in peace and quiet.

'Well so do I,' said Karlson reproachfully. 'Bring on the coffee and offer me a cigar, and let's be civilized, shall we?'

But Uncle Julius shooed him out, and that made Miss Crawley give a satisfied laugh. She clearly thought she had won this one.

'I'm not standing for this,' said Karlson. 'I shall have to show them.'

And the next morning, when Uncle Julius was at the doctor's and Miss Crawley had gone to the big indoor market to buy fish, Karlson flew down to Smidge clutching a big brace drill. Smidge had seen it hanging on the wall up at Karlson's, and he wondered what Karlson was planning to use it for. But just then they heard the thud of the letterbox, and Smidge ran to look. There were two postcards on the front door mat, one from Seb and one from Sally. Smidge was very pleased, and spent ages reading his cards, and by the time he had finished, Karlson had finished too. He had drilled a peephole, right through the door.

'Oh, Karlson, no,' said Smidge in alarm. 'You're not to drill holes . . . why did you do that?'

'So I can see what they're up to, of course,' said Karlson.

'Shame on you,' said Smidge. 'Mum says we mustn't ever look through keyholes.'

'She's got sense, your mum,' said Karlson. 'She's quite right. Keyholes are supposed to have keys in, you can tell that from the way the word sounds. But this happens to be a peephole. You're a clever boy, so I bet you can tell from the word what one of those is for . . . Yes, quite right,' he said, before Smidge had time to answer.

He took a lump of old chewing gum out of his mouth and used it to plug the hole so it wouldn't show.

'Whoop, whoop,' he said. 'It's a long time since we had an evening's fun, but tonight we might be in luck again.'

Then Karlson flew home with his brace drill.

'I've got a few bits of business to take care of,' he said. 'But I'll be back when I smell the fish frying.'

'What sort of business?' asked Smidge.

'One short, sharp bit of business, so at least I've got some money for stamps,' said Karlson. And off he flew.

But he was as good as his word and came back when he smelled the fish frying, and at dinner he was in high spirits. He took a five öre piece out of his pocket and put it in Miss Crawley's hand.

'Here's a little something to cheer you up,' he said. 'Buy yourself some trinket to wear round your neck, or whatever you like!'

Miss Crawley flung down the coin.

'I'll trinket you, however big you think you are,' she said. But just then Uncle Julius came along, and Miss Crawley clearly didn't want him to catch her trinketing Karlson.

'Oh no, because she goes all sweet and swoony as soon as Uncle Julius is anywhere near,' Karlson said to Smidge afterwards. Miss Crawley and Uncle Julius had already gone into the sitting room to have their coffee together as usual, just the two of them.

'Now we'll see just how awful they can really be,' said Karlson. 'I'll have one last try at doing things the friendly way, but then I shall start tirritating them without mercy.'

To Smidge's surprise, he produced a cigar from his breast pocket. He lit it, and then knocked on the door. Nobody called 'Come in', but Karlson went in anyway, puffing busily on his cigar.

'Excuse me, this is the smoking room, isn't it?' he said. 'So I presume I can smoke my cigar here!'

But this made Uncle Julius really lose his temper with Karlson. He snatched away the cigar and broke it in two, and said if he ever saw Karlson smoking again, Karlson would get a box on the ears he'd never forget, and wouldn't ever be allowed to play with Smidge again, Uncle Julius would make sure of that, he said.

Karlson's bottom lip began to quiver, his eyes filled with tears and he aimed an angry little kick at Uncle Julius.

'And there was me bothering to be nice to you day after day, you stupid man,' he said with a glare that showed what he really thought of Uncle Julius.

But Uncle Julius bundled him out of the room, the door was pulled shut again, and what was more they could hear Uncle Julius bolting it. No one had ever done that before.

'See what I mean?' said Karlson to Smidge. 'There's nothing for it but tirritation now.'

Then he thumped on the door with his fist and shouted:

'*And* you've ruined my expensive cigar, you stupid man!'

But then he put his hand in his trouser pocket and jingled something. It sounded like money; goodness gracious, it sounded like five öre coins, a whole lot of them.

'Good job I'm rich,' he said, and that made Smidge worried.

'Where did you get all that money from?'

Karlson gave a secretive wink.

'You'll find out tomorrow,' he said.

That made Smidge even more anxious. What if Karlson had gone out and pinched the money from somewhere? That would mean he was no better than Spike and Rollo. Oh dear, what if Karlson turned out to be an expert at more than just apple additionating, Smidge began to wonder. But he couldn't worry about it any more just now, because Karlson had started quietly and carefully prising the lump of chewing gum out of the peephole.

'There,' he said, and put his eye to the hole. But then he suddenly shrank back, as if he had seen something shocking.

'Well, they've got a cheek!' he said.

'What are they doing?' asked Smidge, curious to know.

'That's what I'd like to know, too,' said Karlson. 'But they've moved, the sneaky rascals!'

Uncle Julius and Miss Crawley always sat on a little sofa that could be very clearly seen through the peephole, and that's where they had been sitting when Karlson went in with his cigar. But they weren't sitting there any longer. Smidge could see this, when he took a peep for himself. They must have moved to the sofa over by the window, and that was really sly and crafty of them, Karlson said. People with any manners always sit where you can see them through keyholes *or* peepholes, he declared.

Poor Karlson, he flopped down onto a chair in the

hall and stared glumly into the distance. For once
he seemed to have given up. His brilliant peephole
plan had come to nothing, and it was hard!

'Come on,' he said in the end. 'Let's go into your
room and see what we can find. Maybe you've got a
few good tirritation bits and bobs among all your
rubbish.'

Karlson spent ages rummaging in Smidge's cup-
boards and drawers without finding anything to
tirritate with, but he suddenly gave a whistle and
pulled out a length of glass tubing, which Smidge
used as a peashooter.

'This is just the sort of thing for a bit,' he said with satisfaction, 'if I can only find a bob to go with it!'

And he did find a bob, a really excellent one. It was a limp little rubber balloon, the sort you can blow up big and round.

'Whoop, whoop,' said Karlson, his pudgy hands trembling eagerly as he slipped the neck of the balloon over one end of the glass tube. Then he put his mouth to the other end of the tube and blew up the balloon, and gave a chuckle of delight as he saw the ugly face that was printed in black on the yellow balloon swelling up larger and larger as he blew.

'I think it's meant to be the man in the moon,' said Smidge.

'It doesn't matter what it's meant to be,' said Karlson, letting the air out of the balloon again, 'as long as it works for tirritating with.'

And it certainly did. It worked very well indeed, even though Smidge had such fits of the giggles that he almost spoilt everything.

'Whoop, whoop,' said Karlson, carefully poking the glass tube with the limp little balloon on the

end through the peephole. Then he blew down the tube with all his might, and Smidge stood beside him, giggling. Oh, how he wished he could be sitting in there on the sofa with Miss Crawley and Uncle Julius and suddenly see a man in the moon ballooning up in all his glory, not in the sky where a man in the moon *ought* to be, but somewhere in the shadows over by the door. It never got really dark at this time of year, but it was definitely dusky enough in the sitting room to make an out-of-place moon like this one look weird and scary, Smidge thought.

'I've got to do the ghostly groans,' said Karlson. 'You do the blowing for a bit, so the balloon doesn't go down!'

So Smidge put his mouth to the glass tube and blew obediently, while Karlson started doing his most horrible ghostly groans. That was probably what made the two of them in the sitting room give a start and finally notice the man in the moon, because at last Karlson got the scream he had been waiting for!

'Scream away,' said Karlson delightedly, but then he whispered, 'Quick, there's no time to lose!'

He let the air out of the balloon. There was a little raspberry sound as it went down and shrank back into a limp bit of rubber, which Karlson swiftly pulled back through the peephole, and just as swiftly plugged the hole with a fresh piece of chewing gum before diving straight under the hall table into his usual hiding place, with Smidge scurrying after him as fast as he could.

A second later they heard the bolt being drawn back; then the door opened and Miss Crawley stuck her head out.

'It must just have been the children, after all,' she said.

But Uncle Julius, standing right behind her, protested hotly.

'How many times have I got to tell you that the whole of fairyland is full of mystical beings, and it's only mystical beings that can float straight through closed doors, don't you see?'

Miss Crawley softened, and said of course she realized that, now she came to think about it. But she obviously didn't want any mystical beings from fairyland spoiling her evening coffee with Uncle Julius, because she soon managed to coax him back to the sofa again. And that left Karlson and Smidge sitting in the hall with a closed door to look at, which wasn't much fun, thought Smidge. And Karlson must have thought so, too. Yes, he most certainly did!

Their thoughts were interrupted by the ring of the telephone. Smidge answered. It was a woman's voice, asking to speak to Miss Crawley. Smidge realized it must be Frida in Frey Street, and he was glad, though he knew he shouldn't be. Now he was entitled to go and disturb Miss Crawley as much as he wanted, and although he was a kindly little boy, he rather liked the idea.

'Telephone for Miss Crawley,' he shouted, and thumped on the door.

But it didn't do him any good.

'Tell them I'm busy,' Miss Crawley shouted back. Neither mystical beings nor Fridas could lure her away from coffee time with Uncle Julius. Smidge went back to the phone and gave Frida the message, but then Frida demanded to know why her sister was so busy and when she could ring again and all sorts of other things. In the end, Smidge said:

'You'd better ask her yourself, in the morning!'

Then he hung up and looked round for Karlson. But Karlson had vanished. Smidge went looking for him, and found him in the kitchen. By the open window, to be exact. Poised on the window ledge astride Mum's best broom, ready to fly off, was something that must be Karlson, although it looked like a little witch or magic troll woman, all black in the face, with a headscarf tied under her chin and a flowery witches' cape round her shoulders—it was Granny's old housecoat, which she had left in the broom cupboard last time she came to stay.

'Oh no, Karlson,' said Smidge anxiously, 'you're not to fly where Uncle Julius can see you any more!'

'I'm not Karlson,' said Karlson in a deep voice. 'I'm a hag, wild and wonderful.'

'A hag?' asked Smidge. 'Is that like a witch?'

'Yes, but worse,' said Karlson. 'Hags are much

more unfriendly. If anyone provokes them, they attack without a second thought!'

'But . . . ' objected Smidge.

'The most dangerous creatures in all fairyland,' declared Karlson. 'And I know of a couple of people who are about to see the hag so close that their hair will stand on end.'

And out into the magical blue twilight flew the hag. Smidge just stood there, not knowing what to do, but then he had an idea. He ran into Seb's room. From there he would have as good a view of the flying hag as Miss Crawley and Uncle Julius in the sitting room.

It was a bit stuffy in the room, so Smidge opened the window. He looked out, and saw that the sitting room window was open, too—open to the summer night and to fairyland! And Miss Crawley and Uncle Julius were sitting inside right now, not even realizing there *was* such a thing as a hag, poor people, thought Smidge. They were so close to him that he could hear their voices as a sort of murmur, but what a shame he couldn't see them as well!

He could see the hag, though. Imagine if he hadn't known it was only Karlson, and not a real hag: his blood would have run cold, he was convinced of it, because it's really creepy when a hag comes flying in like that. It was enough to make anybody believe in fairyland, thought Smidge.

The hag swept past the sitting room window several times, and looked in. Whatever she saw seemed to surprise and even annoy her, because she shook her head several times. She still hadn't noticed Smidge at the other window, and he didn't dare call out. But he waved wildly, and then the hag spotted him. She waved back, and her black face lit up in a broad grin.

Uncle Julius and Miss Crawley couldn't have seen her, since their mumbling voices were carrying on so calmly, thought Smidge. But then it let rip . . . a scream cutting suddenly through the peace and quiet of the summer evening. She screamed, the hag, oh dear, she screamed like a . . . well, like a hag, I suppose, because it wasn't like any scream Smidge had ever heard in his life, and it sounded as if it could have come straight from fairyland.

There was no more mumbling from the sitting room, just total silence.

Then the hag came whizzing in through the window to Smidge, and quick as a flash she tore off her headscarf and housecoat and wiped her sooty face on Seb's curtains, and then there was no hag any more, just Karlson, who swiftly shoved the clothes and the broom and the whole hagerama under Seb's bed.

'Do you know what,' said Karlson, bounding angrily up to Smidge, 'it should be against the law for old people to carry on like that.'

'Like what? What were they doing?' asked Smidge.

Karlson shook his head in annoyance.

'He was holding her hand! He was sitting there holding her hand! Her, Creepy Crawley, what do you say to that?'

Karlson was staring at Smidge as if he expected Smidge to fall down in a faint of sheer astonishment, and when he didn't, Karlson bellowed:

'Did you hear what I said? They were sitting there holding hands! How soppy can people get?'

KARLSON IS THE WORLD'S RICHEST MAN

Smidge would never forget the day that followed. He woke up early, all by himself. There were no shouts from the world's best Karlson to rouse him. Strange, thought Smidge, and then he padded out to the hall to fetch the newspaper. He wanted to read the cartoon strips in peace, before Uncle Julius came along, wanting the paper.

But no cartoon strips got read that day. Poor Smidge, he didn't get any further than the front page of the paper. Because his eye was drawn to a giant headline that brought him out in a sweat.

MYSTERY SOLVED—NOT A SPY
AFTER ALL

it said.

Underneath was a picture of Västerbro Bridge, and flying above it—there was no mistaking him—flying above it was Karlson. There was a close-up of him, too, standing there smirking, showing off his collapsible propeller and his starting button, the one on his tummy.

Smidge read it, and what he read made him cry.

We received a remarkable visit at our offices yesterday. A handsome, thoroughly clever, perfectly plump man in his prime—as he described himself—came in to claim our ten thousand kronor reward. He, and he alone, was the mystery flying object of the Vasa district, he declared, but he said he was not a spy, and we believe him. 'I only spy on people like Creepy Crawley and Jules the Elf,' he said. It all sounded very childish and innocent, and as far as we can tell, this 'spy' is just an unusually tubby little schoolboy—best in the class, he claims—but this boy has something any child would envy: a little motor that means he is able to fly, as you can see from the picture. The motor was made by the world's best inventor, the boy claimed, but he was unwilling to give further details. We pointed out to him that the inventor could become a multi-millionaire, if he started mass-producing the motor, but the boy responded: 'No thanks, we don't want the air full of flying kids. It's just right with me and Smidge!'

Here, Smidge did smile a bit—just think, Karlson only wanted to go flying with him, after all, not with anyone else!—but then he gave a little sob and went on reading.

The boy didn't seem quite normal, it must be said. He spoke in a confused manner, gave very strange answers to our questions, and did not even want to tell us his parents' names. 'Ma's a mummy and Pa's the Sandman,' he finally told us, but we could get no more out of him. Sandman sounds a bit foreign, so maybe the boy's father is a foreigner, but he seems to be a flying ace, at any rate, as far as we could gather from the boy's wittering. And his father's enthusiasm for flying has clearly been inherited by the son.

The boy insisted on claiming his reward at once. 'I'm the one who's to have it, not Spike or Rollo or any other thuggy thief,' he said. And he wanted the whole lot in five öre pieces, 'Because they're the only real money,' he said. He left us with his pockets stuffed full of small coins. He is coming to fetch the rest with a wheelbarrow as soon as he can. 'And don't go losing my money, or the hag will come and get you,' he said. He was certainly an entertaining visitor, even if it was hard to make out what he meant. 'Remember you've only paid for about one big toe so far,' were his final words, and then he flew out of the window and disappeared in the direction of Vasa.

Oddly enough, the boy is not called Sandman like his father—he refused to explain this either—and he insisted he did not want his own name in the paper, 'Because Smidge won't like it,' he said. He seemed most concerned about this person called Smidge, who may be his brother. So we can't reveal the boy's name, though we can say that it starts with 'Karl' and ends with 'son'. But if someone doesn't want his name in the papers, then he is perfectly entitled, we think, to have his way. That is why we have referred to the boy as just 'the boy', and not 'Karlson', which is his actual name.

'He seemed most concerned about this person called Smidge, who may be his brother,' mumbled Smidge, and gave another snuffly little sob. But then he went to the bell system and tugged angrily on the cord, the signal that meant 'Come here!'

And Karlson came. He whirred in through the window, as merry and giddy as a bumblebee.

'Anything special in the paper today?' he asked roguishly, as he dug up the peach stone. 'Read it out if there does happen to be anything interesting!'

'You've gone too far this time,' said Smidge. 'Don't you see you've ruined everything now? They'll never leave us alone, you and me.'

'Who wants to be left alone?' said Karlson, wiping the soil off his hands onto Smidge's pyjamas. 'It's got to be heysan and hopsan and hi, or you can count me out, just so you know. Now come on, read me something!'

So while Karlson flew to and fro in front of the mirror and admired himself, Smidge read to him. He missed out the bits like 'unusually tubby' and anything else that might annoy Karlson, but he read the rest of it from start to finish, and Karlson puffed up with delight.

'Entertaining visitor, that's me all right—you know, they tell nothing but the truth in that newspaper.'

'He seemed most concerned about this person called Smidge,' read Smidge, and gave Karlson a shy look. 'Is that the truth, too?'

Karlson stopped in mid-air to think about it.

'Yes, oddly enough,' he admitted, slightly unwillingly. 'Just imagine anybody being bothered about a silly little boy like you! It's my goodness coming through, of course, because I'm the world's goodest, kindest Karlson . . . go on reading!'

But Smidge couldn't go on before he'd swallowed the lump in his throat—just think, it was true that Karlson liked him after all, so he didn't really care about anything else!

'It was just as well I told them that about my name, and not putting it in the paper,' said Karlson.

'I only said it for your sake, because I know you want to keep me top, top secret.'

Then he grabbed hold of the paper and took a long, loving look at the two photographs.

'It's incredible how handsome I am,' he said. 'And how perfectly plump, it's incredible, just look!'

He held the paper under Smidge's nose. But then he whisked it away again and gave his picture, the one of him showing off his starting button, a smacking kiss,

'Whoop whoop, the very sight of me makes me feel like shouting hurrah!' he said.

But Smidge snatched the paper back from him.

'We must make sure Miss Crawley and Uncle Julius don't see this, at any rate,' he said. 'They mustn't ever, ever see it!'

He took the paper over to his desk and stuffed it as deep into the drawer as he could. The next minute, Uncle Julius stuck his nose into the room and asked:

'Have you got the paper, Smidge?'

Smidge shook his head.

'No, I haven't!'

After all, he hadn't *got* it if it was in the desk drawer, he explained to Karlson afterwards.

Uncle Julius didn't seem particularly worried about the newspaper, in any case. He must have had something else on his mind, and it must have been something nice, because he seemed in a particularly happy mood. And he had to get off to the doctor's, anyway. It was his last appointment. Because in a few hours' time Uncle Julius would be setting off home across Sweden to Västergötland.

Miss Crawley helped him on with his coat, and Smidge and Karlson could hear her giving him instructions. He was to keep his coat done up at the neck and watch out for cars in the street and not smoke so early in the day.

'What's got into Creepy Crawley?' said Karlson. 'Does she think they're married or something?'

This was certainly turning out to be a day of surprises! Uncle Julius was hardly out of the door before Miss Crawley dashed to the phone and they heard her making a call. And because she was speaking in such a loud voice, the two of them could hear everything she said.

'Hello, Frida, is that you?' she said heartily. 'How are you? Still got your nose on? . . . Ah, right, but listen: there's no need for you to worry about *my* nose any more, because I'm planning on taking it with me to Västergötland, since I'm moving down there, you see . . . No, not as a housekeeper, I'm getting married, ugly though I may be, what do you say to that? . . . Yes, of course I'll tell you: to Mr Julius Janson himself . . . Yes indeed, it's as good as Mrs Janson you're talking to, Frida dear . . . Oh dear, that's taken you by surprise, I can hear you crying . . . no, no, Frida, don't howl, I'm sure you can pick up another burglar without too much trouble . . . Well, I mustn't go on, my fiancé will be back any time now ... . I'll tell you all about it later, Frida dear.'

Karlson stared wide-eyed at Smidge.

'Isn't there some nasty-tasting, quick-working medicine for people who've gone off their heads?' he asked. 'Because if there is, we need to pour a huge, enormous dose of it into Uncle Julius right away!'

But Smidge hadn't heard of any medicine like

that. Karlson gave a sigh of sympathy, and when Uncle Julius got back from the doctor's, Karlson sidled up to him and pressed a five öre piece into his hand.

'What's this for?' asked Uncle Julius.

'Buy something to cheer you up,' said Karlson gravely. 'You need it.'

Uncle Julius thanked him, but said he was so pleased with life that he didn't need any five öre pieces to cheer him up.

'Though you boys will be sorry, of course, to hear that I'm taking Aunt Hilda away from you.'

'Aunt Hilda,' said Karlson, 'who the dickens is she?'

And when Smidge explained it to him, he had a good, long laugh.

But Uncle Julius went on talking about how happy he was. He would never forget this visit, he said. First, fairyland had been revealed to him in such a wonderful way! Of course it scared you sometimes, when witches came flying through the window, he wouldn't deny it, but . . .

'Not witches,' said Karlson. 'Hags, wild and quite horribly terrifying!'

But it did make you realize that you lived in the same world as your ancestors, Uncle Julius went on, and he liked it there, he said. Because the best thing of all that this visit had given him was a fairytale princess of his own, called Hilda, and now there was going to be a wedding!

'A fairytale princess called Hilda,' said Karlson, his eyes sparkling. He laughed for a long time, then looked at Uncle Julius and shook his head, and started laughing again.

Miss Crawley was stomping about in the kitchen, happier than Smidge had ever seen her.

'I like witches, too,' she said, 'because if that foul thing hadn't come flying past the window and scared us yesterday evening, then you'd never have thrown yourself into my arms, Julius, and this would never have happened.'

Karlson gave a start.

'Well I like that,' he began indignantly, but then he just shrugged his shoulders. 'Still, that's a mere trifle,' he said. 'Though I don't think we'll be having any more hags in this part of town.'

Miss Crawley, meanwhile, was simply getting happier and happier, the more she thought about the wedding.

'You can be a page boy, Smidge,' she said, patting him on the cheek. 'I'll make you a little suit of black velvet. Just think how sweet you'll look!'

Smidge shuddered . . . a black velvet suit, Kris and Jemima would laugh themselves sick!

But Karlson wasn't laughing, he was angry.

'You can count me out if I can't be a page boy as well,' he said. 'And I want to wear a black velvet suit and be sweet, too, or you can count me out!'

Then it was Miss Crawley's turn to laugh.

'A fine wedding it would be, if we let *you* into the church.'

'That's exactly what I think,' said Karlson eagerly. 'I could stand behind you in my black velvet suit and waggle my ears the whole time and give a gun salute every now and then, because you have to have salutes at weddings!'

Uncle Julius, who was so happy and wanted everybody else to be in a good mood too, said that of course Karlson could come. But then Miss Crawley said that if she had to have Karlson as a page boy, she'd rather not get married at all.

The day reached evening, as all days do. Smidge sat up on Karlson's front steps and watched the night draw in and the lights start to go on round about, all over Vasa and all over Stockholm, as far as his eyes could see.

Yes, it was evening now, and here he sat with Karlson beside him, which was undeniably nice. Somewhere down in Västergötland, a train was just steaming into a little station and Uncle Julius was getting off. Somewhere out in the Baltic Sea, a white steamer was heading home to Stockholm with Mum and Dad on board. Miss Crawley was over at Frey Street, cheering up Frida. Bumble had snuggled down in his basket for the night. But up here on the roof sat Smidge with his best friend beside him, and they were tucking into a big bagful of buns, Miss Crawley's yummy, freshly baked buns, and that was great. But Smidge looked worried, even so. There was never any peace if you were Karlson's best friend.

'I've done my best to get you through it all safely,' said Smidge. 'I've kept watch over you, I really have. But I just don't know what's going to happen now.'

Karlson took another bun from the bag and swallowed it whole.

'Don't be daft! I mean to say, they can't hand me in to the paper and get loads of five öre pieces, I've foiled them there, so now they'll lose interest, you know, Spike and Rollo and the whole bunch!'

Smidge helped himself to another bun, too, and took a thoughtful bite.

'You're the one who's daft,' he said. 'The whole district is bound to be crawling with people even so, silly idiots who want to see you fly or try to steal your motor and all sorts of stuff.'

Karlson beamed.

'Do you really think so? Well, if you're right, maybe we can have an evening's fun now and then, after all.'

'An evening's fun?' said Smidge indignantly. 'We'll never have a minute's peace, like I said, either of us.'

Karlson beamed even more brightly.

'Do you really think so? Well, let's hope you're right.'

That made Smidge really cross.

'But how will you cope?' he demanded. 'How will you cope, if swarms of people turn up here?'

Karlson put his head on one side and gave Smidge a conspiratorial look.

'There are three ways, you know that. Tirritation, jiggery-pokery, and figuration. And I plan on using all three, the whole lot.'

He looked so sly that Smidge had to laugh, in spite of himself. He gave a giggle, just a quiet little giggle at first, but then masses of giggle bubbled up inside him, and the more he giggled, the more delighted Karlson grew.

'Whoop, whoop,' he said, and gave Smidge such a shove that he almost fell down the steps. That made Smidge giggle even more, and think that maybe the real fun was just about to start.

But Karlson sat there on the steps, looking affectionately at a little pair of blackened big toes sticking out of his holey socks.

'No, I'm not selling these,' he said. 'Don't nag me

about it any more, Smidge! Just don't, because these big toes are attached to the world's richest man and they're not for sale any more.'

He put his hand in his pocket and happily jingled his hoard of five öre coins.

'Whoop, whoop, a rich, handsome, thoroughly clever, perfectly plump man in his prime, that's me. The world's best Karlson in every possible way, do you see, Smidge?'

'Yes,' said Smidge.

But there was more in Karlson's pockets than just coins: there was a little pistol, too, and before Smidge could stop him, a shot rang out that echoed all round Vasa.

Here we go, thought Smidge, as he saw windows opening in all the houses around them, and heard agitated voices.

As for Karlson, he burst into song, wiggling his two little black big toes in time to the beat:

It's got to go bang and I've got to have fun
With a tralala and a tumty tum
And what is a birthday without a bun?

With a tralala and a tumty tum.
It's got to be heysan and hopsan and hi,
And everyone's s'posed to be nice as pie
With a whoop-de-whoop
And a loop the loop
And a tumty tumty tum.

ASTRID LINDGREN

Astrid Lindgren was born in Vimmerby, Sweden in 1907. In the course of her life she wrote over 40 books for children, and has sold over 145 million copies worldwide. She once commented, 'I write to amuse the child within me, and can only hope that other children may have some fun that way too.'

Many of Astrid Lindgren's stories are based upon her memories of childhood and they are filled with lively and unconventional characters. Perhaps the best known is *Pippi Longstocking*, first published in Sweden in 1945. It was an immediate success, and was published in England in 1954.

Awards for Astrid Lindgren's writing include the prestigious Hans Christian Andersen Award and the International Book Award. In 1989 a theme park dedicated to her—Astrid Lindgren *Värld* (Astrid Lindgren World)—was opened in Vimmerby. She died in 2002 at the age of 94.